MARRIED
SEX

MARRIED
S/E/X

A LOVE STORY

JESSE KORNBLUTH

OPEN ROAD
INTEGRATED MEDIA
NEW YORK

Excerpt from "Woman" from *The Complete Poems* by Randall Jarrell copyright © 1969, renewed 1997 by Mary von S. Jarrell, reprinted by permission of Farrar, Straus and Giroux, LLC.

Lyrics from "Joy to You Baby" written by Josh Ritter, reprinted by permission of Rural Songs.

Cover design by Andy Ross

978-1-5040-1125-9

Published in 2015 by Open Road Integrated Media, Inc.
345 Hudson Street
New York, NY 10014
www.openroadmedia.com

To HH

MARRIED
SEX

When, like Disraeli, I murmur
That you are more like a mistress than a wife,
More like an angel than a mistress; when, like Satan,
I hiss in your ear some vile suggestion,
Some delectable abomination,
You smile at me indulgently: "Men, men!"

—"Woman," Randall Jarrell

CHAPTER 1

"The most beautiful woman in the world is a woman reading a book."

I didn't mean to say that. Or anything, really. It just came out—an awkward, schoolboy admission, sincerity gone wrong.

Blair was the woman with the book. She sat on the couch, looking like tens of thousands of New York women who know they're attractive and don't want to have to deal with it every minute of the day. But she was a corporate nun only from a distance. Her straight navy skirt stopped above the knee, emphasizing long, bare runner's legs. And her white silk blouse was unbuttoned just far enough to reveal fairly significant curves.

People who knew her back in Iowa would be stunned to see Blair now. As she stepped into middle age, she had her breasts done. She didn't go too far—just the suggestion of far, the suburbs of appropriateness.

To say I'm interested in those curves is to understate—when it comes to breasts, I'm a first responder.

Blair was ignoring the skirt inching up her thighs and the glass of white wine on the table by her side.

Whatever she was reading, it was serious enough to merit a pencil in her hand.

She finished making a note, looked up, saw me studying her, and had no trouble reading my mind. Her laugh was instant. Also eloquently dismissive. She didn't really need to say "Be a nice boy and let me read." But she did. And then she waved in the direction of the kitchen.

"Dinner in five," I said.

"Ten," she countered, and tapped her pencil on the book. "Pages."

Salad dressed with lemon juice and a chicken breast beaten paper-thin—there are women in New York who consider that a meal. It's not my idea of dinner, and it's nothing I'd cook for anyone I care about. For Blair, I'd made real food: sautéed zucchini to start, served lukewarm with chopped mint and a drizzle of olive oil, then roast chicken with fresh herbs tucked under the skin, and boiled small red potatoes and French beans, both glistening in melted butter.

Calories don't count, especially when you know you're going to burn them off.

Blair read more than ten pages, but I didn't care. While she read, I made unnecessary trips to the living room—"More olives, Blair? Let me refresh that wine"—just to look at her. Not for the outfit, though I find classic and corporate to be oddly hot. I went for the visual of a woman reading a book.

Over the years, I've come to think that the best way to learn about a woman—the best way short of spending a night with her—is to watch her read. When she's deep in a book, you can easily imagine what she was like as a kid, curled up on the porch or in her room, ignoring her mother's call as she races to finish one more chapter, one more page. She's all essence. And what you see there—that's valuable information.

The information here: intensity. Total absorption. This is a woman who can focus on a project long after everyone else has gone home. Or wrap her legs around a lover and, eyes closed, thrust as if her life depended on it.

During the last serious real estate crash, when anyone with a job and some savings could live high above his means, I bought an apartment on the tenth floor at 94th Street and Central Park West. Its special attraction: In late summer and early fall, as the sun sets, the great limestone fortresses across the park begin to transform. From my living room, the heat of the day leaving the park makes the Fifth Avenue buildings look like they're on the far side of a misty valley in Tuscany; the windows in those buildings could be the lights of a distant hill town.

At that hour, in that light, the apartment also glows. And with candles lit in the dining room, time seems to slow. I started the sensual music of Cesária Évora and filled wineglasses with second-growth Bordeaux.

Unoriginal? Worse—corny. But the scene was set.

The aroma of the herbed pan gravy was restaurant-worthy. The wine was so smooth we drank it like water. As we ate, I felt the edges of anticipation moving in.

"What are you reading?"

"Lesley Blanch. *The Wilder Shores of Love.* You've never heard of it. She wrote it in the fifties."

"What's it about?"

"Four Victorian women who went off to live in the Middle East."

"How did you hear about it?"

"It was summer reading for the new First-Year Class."

"And if they don't read it?"

"They'll be embarrassed at my lecture . . . maybe."

This was so like Blair. Conscientious to a fault. Always hoping for the best. There are Barnard deans who attract the cool kids—Blair specializes in the afflicted. She attracts the never-been-away-from-home-befores, the evangelical Christians on their first tour of Gomorrah, the closeted gays. And, behind them, the usual crop of wounded eighteen-year-olds, with their predictable troubles: parents stricken by cancer just weeks after dropping their daughters off, parents who waited until the nest was empty to split up, parents hurt because they're no longer writing every paper.

Blair is also a lecturer in Women's Studies. I'm sure that the first time any number of new Barnard students knock on her door they're expecting a West Side feminist from a time capsule: frizzy-haired, cosmetics-challenged, badly dressed and proud of it. But Blair is more like Gloria Steinem than Betty Friedan. Her hair is professionally streaked, she gets treatments for her skin, and she dresses for her office as if she were going to a C-suite. "Role model" applies here.

"Why this book?"

I sensed a preview of Blair's lecture ahead and poured more wine.

"In an un-liberated era, these women broke the narrow restrictions of their class."

"Forged their own identities," I suggested.

"Went on their own journeys," she said, and we laughed, because Blair knows how that word grates on me. It's stupid to be annoyed by such a little thing, but I seriously think *journey* belongs only in the mouths of Best Supporting Actresses and only when they're accepting their Oscars.

"What's this book say about love?"

"I think I can quote her. 'There are two sorts of romantics: those who love and those who love the adventure of loving.'"

"Which are you?"

Blair didn't hesitate. "Both."

On the far side of dinner a thin joint awaited. Never before, never during—that's just an invitation to gorge. After, it makes apples and cheese seem like a real dessert and coffee like exotic nectar. And it gives definition to an evening; one segment is over, another begins.

It was almost nine o'clock; everyone who was going somewhere tonight was there now. We were going nowhere. Dinner finished and plates pushed aside, we sat at the table, making progress on a second bottle of wine as Otis Redding sang about women who please and tease you, love and wrong you, hope for a little tenderness.

Comfort surrounded us.

I lit the joint and handed it over. Blair inhaled with a ruthless efficiency.

"Somewhere out there," she said when she could hold the smoke no longer, "is a client who would be very disturbed to know you muddy your mind like this."

"Somewhere out there is a client who would love for me to muddy my mind with her."

"Ah yes, the always available divorce lawyer," Blair said, and took another puff.

"I'm far down the list of desirables."

"Not possible."

"Gynecologists. Tennis pros. They're . . . kings."

"True," Blair said. "Here's some consolation: You're above gardeners."

Blair surrendered the joint. Then she looked blank; she'd gone interior. I watched as she tried to follow her thought to its end. But she got lost in the middle—she wasn't getting there anytime soon.

"Blair?"

She blinked and returned to Friday night on Central Park West.

"Sorry," she said. "Where were we?"

"You were in the ozone. I was here, looking at you and thinking about a picture."

"What of?"

"It was after dinner. They've finished the meal, but they're happy to stay at the table and chat. She's smoking a cigarette. He asks her to open her blouse. She does. She's not wearing a bra. She inhales. And just then, he takes . . . one picture. One very memorable picture."

"Helmut Newton," she said. "It's a picture of his wife."

Without prompting, Blair opened more buttons and unhooked a clasp at the front of her bra. Her breasts took center stage: round, almost heavy, the nipples pink and hardening.

"Like this?" she asked.

In a flash, I was up and moving around the table. Blair pushed her chair back. I slipped a finger into her mouth. She licked and sucked it. I removed my finger, circled her lips with it, set it on a nipple, and, slowly, started to make gentle circles. I varied the speed: faster on the way up, a slow graze across the top, a swoop down, a light pinch at the bottom. And again. And again.

My mouth was pressed to her left ear; I tongued it lightly. I could feel Blair arch her back, hear her breathing change. I reached under her skirt, my right hand stroking the inside of her thighs.

My fingertips rested between her legs. Slowly, slowly, I stroked her, up and down, side to side. Her eyes were closed, her arms were limp.

If I had my way, we'd never have made it to the bedroom—I would have pushed plates off the table, undressed Blair right there, and had her standing up. When it was over, I'd have dropped to the floor, panting, head spinning. And I would have been thrilled, because we'd taken all the complexity of a relationship and dialed it down to animal heat.

Blair had more self-control.

"Oh my God, oh my God." Blair gently pushed me away. "Let's go to bed."

In the bedroom, I undressed quickly, carelessly, and lit a candle. The CD player clicked, and we were joined by rum-and-reggae dreamscapes, music that made me picture camels gliding across sand in the moonlight, a woman lowering herself onto a man on a chaise on a Caribbean beach at midnight. Movie music, the soundtrack of lush sex.

I turned to Blair. She was already in bed, face down,

arms at her side. This is a woman who thinks she's carrying five impossible-to-lose extra pounds—all of it in her ass—and who never runs around the reservoir without a sweater tied around her waist as a butt cover. Which is madness; those five pounds are her glory. But face down on the bed—here was a different Blair, free and loose.

Kneeling beside her, I stroked her ass, my hand drifting across the line where buttock met thigh. Blair shivered.

"So hot," she whispered.

But although Blair tensed, although a series of small external orgasms had her moaning, that large, final, internal spasm eluded her.

There are nights when nothing gets your lover there, when you're drenched with sweat and she says, "Come . . . you come." And because you've done your best and it's not in any way a defeat, you lock your hands on her wrists and let go.

And then there are nights when you're so committed to her orgasm that you'll run through the catalogue of positions and techniques.

This was one of those nights.

Blair's breath was ragged. She was digging her nails into my back. Attention and technique had become just . . . activity.

"Get off," she ordered, and when I wasn't fast enough,

she pushed my chest. I pulled out, and we reached for the water glasses we keep on our night tables. Like boxers between rounds.

"Now what?" I asked, panting.

"I take care of you," Blair said.

Blair circled her hand around me, tugging gently, her tongue barely touching me. If I had died just then, it would have been from excessive joy.

This is what it's like to be a woman, I thought, and surrendered to being unmanned. Blair glowed with power, and I glowed with powerlessness, and then the wine and the smoke and the woman converged. I saw colors—gold and royal purple—and then my head emptied of everything.

A violent thrust. I grabbed her head. But I've never liked finishing that way—it's too much like a ritual in a porn movie, too disrespectful, too raw—and, somehow, I unhooked from Blair, threw her on her back, called her *darling, dearest, only.*

With that, bliss flooded through me, and I reared back one final time and drained myself into my beloved wife of twenty years.

CHAPTER 2

At nine in the morning on the second Monday in September, I knew—as I've known for a decade now—exactly where my law partner was and what she was doing.

Victoria Denham was in Wainscott, at her house overlooking Georgica Pond. In the Hamptons, it doesn't get better than that. Her neighbors include Steven Spielberg, Martha Stewart, and so many Wall Street executives that cynics call it "Goldman Pond." But these residents shrewdly follow tradition and call their mansions "cottages."

Victoria's house is a real cottage, an ivy-covered bungalow begging for an upgrade it will never get. She doesn't care. For her, the house is all about the view from her picture window—a large bathtub of a pond separated from the ocean by a thin strip of beach, and the ocean beyond.

Water, sand, water, sky: the most privileged view in the Hamptons.

Victoria bought her house in 1980, and not because she has a knack for real estate. She rows. A big-ass rowboat in the beginning. Then a canoe. Now she's got an Ocean Shell—a light but solid boat that's nothing like the feather-weight arrows you see in regattas—that she drags from her ragged lawn to the pond. A dozen strokes take her across the pond to the beach. Then she hauls her boat over a few yards of sand to the ocean and sets off, parallel to the shore, toward East Hampton.

You can do that—row in the Atlantic—in September.

Most mornings, the ocean's dead calm, flat as the pond. The sun is gentle, and there isn't a hint of breeze. It's the best time of the year, made even better by the general absence of New Yorkers—only the very rich or indolent can be out here to enjoy it.

Victoria isn't rich or indolent, just old-fashioned New England practical. When she graduated from law school, representing women in divorce cases was like Atticus Finch defending a black man in *To Kill a Mockingbird*—going in, you knew you were going to lose. That didn't bother her at all; for Victoria, law was simply the quickest way of chang-ing the world for women. And thanks to the prodding and lobbying of lawyers like Victoria, it became possible to build a practice—and make a nice living—getting big settlements for women, especially if the women were married to rich men on the Upper East Side of Manhattan.

Unlocking wealth was the least of it for Victoria. From the beginning, she took on unprofitable clients—women in jail, women on welfare, women in shelters for the battered and broken. She got them divorced, and she helped them with appeals and parole, and, even more remarkable, she hired them. For most of the last two decades, Victoria's receptionist has been a woman so well dressed and soft-spoken you'd never guess she'd escaped an abusive man or spent a decade in jail for larceny.

Every few years, *New York* magazine runs a feature called "New York's Best Divorce Lawyers." Ten years ago, my cousin the journalist was assigned to write it. He called Victoria. She asked who else was being considered for the list. He produced the usual names. She suggested some lawyers who represented poor and beaten women. "Talk to a few of them," she said. "Then call me back."

My cousin didn't reach out to those lawyers. And he didn't connect again with Victoria. But he told me about the conversation, and I got a picture of Victoria that was almost exactly who she turned out to be: savvy and openhearted, cynical and pure, knowledgeable about the man-woman game and happily retired from that messy business—a mass of interesting contradictions.

I'd spent a few unhappy years in a big corporate office. Family law struck me as a better solution than leaving the law entirely. I called Victoria.

My interview began with an excruciatingly long silence, as Victoria did what, in the old days, would have been called "taking my measure." She wasn't shy about it—she sat next to me on the couch and looked me over as if I were a race-horse she might want to claim. I would not be surprised if she knew my dark gray two-button suit and pale blue shirt came from Brooks Brothers, that my black knit tie was Paul Stuart, and that my loafers might have been made by Lobb but weren't. Clearly, someone along the way had taught me the wisdom of a low profile. And for Victoria, that was all the information she needed for a psychological snapshot: Brooklyn-born Jew, desperate to assimilate.

What followed—our actual conversation—was brief. A few weeks later, I joined the firm. We discovered we were good together. In a year, I was Victoria's partner.

Considering the nastiness of our profession, our practice

is unnaturally civilized. Before townhouses became prized real estate, Victoria bought a brownstone in the East 80s between Madison and Park. She lives on the third floor and rents out the fourth; we work on the first two. We're a small crew: Victoria; me; the receptionist; Gladys, the paralegal, who learned her trade in jail and has been on Victoria's payroll since the day of her release; and, as needed, J. T. Schmidt, a German émigré, who became Victoria's investigator in some distant, unspecified year. We call him Reboot because he seems to erase his memory every night.

Now Victoria is working less, and I handle the cases she doesn't want. And when business is slow at Denham and Greenfield—and it's generally slow in the fall because Wall Street wives who have made it through the summer without filing for divorce tend to hang on to their marriages until their husbands collect their bonuses—she takes a few extra weeks at the beach.

But she isn't really away. The first phone call of the day? Victoria, always.

"Da-vid."

My name is always two words with Victoria.

I could hear her steady strokes and metronomic breathing through the cell phone clipped to her waist, and I smiled. A world that has a seventy-year-old woman with more than a passing resemblance to Vanessa Redgrave rowing steadily toward Europe—I call that a good world.

"How's the water today, V?"

Her name is always reduced to an initial in my mouth.

"Flat enough to walk on. And slated to continue."

"Happy to hear it. Staying on?"

"Depends," she said. "What's new?"

"Mary Arnold's husband announced he's moving the family to Umbria for a year."

"What did Mary say?"

"She's going with him."

"She can't think there's a hunky Italian lover waiting for her."

"She left a message. I don't think she wanted our opinion."

"Better yet. What else?"

"Amanda Carpenter called in."

"She made weight?"

"Ninety-nine."

Amanda Carpenter married a man who can't be seen with a woman who weighs more than a hundred pounds. Every Monday morning, by the terms of their prenup, she goes to her husband's doctor and weighs in. She always makes it. You would too if you ate cotton balls for lunch and downed a dozen Diet Cokes a day. But she pays a price. Because no fat passes her lips, she's estrogen-deprived and her chin has sprouted dark hairs, and because she's bulimic, the acid in her vomit is stripping the enamel from her teeth. Why does she submit to this? Although she looks as if she were born in purple, her father is a firefighter and her mother has a chronic disease. Like a character in an Edith Wharton novel, she sacrificed herself on the altar of money. Her husband is rich and social, and, dammit, he wants a wife who looks the part. Amanda knows her marriage is in no way secure, so she hired us to look over the doctor's shoulder.

"Also, Reboot tracked down the manager of that club in Paris. The guy remembers seeing the Stonebachs. He'll give us a deposition."

"Excellent."

Better than that, really. Richard Stonebach is a big-shot political fund-raiser. His new wife—his fourth—came to us right after the honeymoon. As she tells it, his idea of a good start to a marriage was to take her to Paris, bring her to a sex club, and let her watch him get a blow job. Now she wants an annulment and—prenup be damned—a settlement. With a deposition from the manager of that club, Stonebach's choices are a generous good-bye or a story on Page Six.

"What's your week like?" Victoria asked.

"The biggest thing on my calendar is an opening at an art gallery."

"Who's the artist?"

"The Greta Garbo of photography."

"How's her marriage?"

"Trolling for clients, V?"

"As a matter of fact, I went out for dinner over the weekend and came back with one."

"What's she like?"

"In addition to sixty million dollars, she wants half of the frequent flyer miles. Very adamant about that."

"Oh, dear," I said, because I've seen enough vengeful women to know them as unbearable and, in our partnership, always mine to represent. Revenge starts with the frequent flyer miles; it doesn't end until she gets a share of the apartment where the husband meets his mistress.

"So . . . Garbo with a camera . . . Blair going?"

"No."

"Watch yourself, young man."

And Victoria was gone. She hates good-byes.

CHAPTER 3

Jean Coin's photographs are monumental: five feet by five feet. At that scale, a picture of rolled hay bales is close to life-size. Larger objects—rock formations, waterfalls, the edges of a slate roof in rural France—come at you in such sharp focus you feel they want to push through the surface of the paper. I can understand why some people are threatened by these images; they're stark, black-and-white assaults.

I'd love to own one of Jean Coin's pictures, but even the smallest is so big it would dwarf everything in our living room. And even the smallest is expensive. So I enjoy them, every few years, at her dealer's gallery.

The opening was mobbed. I bobbed and weaved through the crowd, snatching a glimpse of a picture, shaking hands, and getting air-kissed by casual friends and former clients. Years of experience at gallery openings led me toward the back office, where, more often than not, you can see the multiples stacked up or find a few pictures that didn't make it into the show. There were people here too, but the groups were smaller, the conversations less buoyant. The crowd cleared out, and for what seemed like an entire minute, I stood alone with a photograph of cliffs in the Dordogne.

And then I wasn't alone. Joining me at the picture was a seriously attractive woman in a starched white shirt, faded Levis, and moccasins. She wasn't lightly bronzed but actually tanned, with hair lightened by the sun. She looked as if she'd spent the summer in a sailboat and had docked just five minutes ago.

There are no more than a dozen photographs of Jean Coin and fewer interviews. Anyone who knew anything about her would have said she was probably half a world away. But here she was. Not happy. Oh, very much not happy—scowling.

"I'm surprised to see you here," I said. "All these people . . ."

"I'm leaving as soon as I figure out what to do with this picture."

"I'm going to guess: You only see the flaws?"

"Cavemen once made their homes there," she said, pointing at a terraced area on the cliffs. "You should feel their presence. Or absence." She pointed lower. "Down here . . . a river to fish in. Do you sense anything swimming? I don't. Farther over are fields where deer grazed, fruit trees growing wild . . . but the picture indicates none of that. It's a dead landscape. And that was not my point."

"How many of these pictures miss the point?"

"Really, only this. It's just . . . wrong."

I'm not awestruck in the presence of artists—a few of the most successful have been our clients—but I would have expected Jean Coin to be remote, even hostile. So far, she was accessible and engaging. I pressed on.

"Your fans disagree."

"Marketing," she said. "Image."

"Why aren't you out there?" I asked, gesturing toward the crowd in the next room.

"You think I came to see how they're selling?"

"It's only natural."

"You don't understand," she said. "My mission is last-minute quality control." And then, almost whispering: "I never know if people think my pictures are worth owning."

Was it possible that Jean Coin had self-esteem issues?

"You set the bar high."

She didn't find that worthy of a response. A change of topic seemed smart.

"Why are there never any people in your pictures?"

She laughed. "Are you going to kiss every cliché on the mouth?"

"Seriously, why do you think that is?" I asked.

"*Seriously?* What is this—an interview?"

"I'm not a writer."

"You collect?"

"School bills."

She gave me a look that said, I'm not kidding around here, I'm taking you for someone of intelligence. That intensity aimed directly at me made me feel something—a perceptible change in the conversational climate, like a blast of oxygen.

"Seriously," I said. "Tell me why there are no people in your pictures."

She gestured to a bench, and we sat. The gallery opening seemed far away.

"What's your theory?" she asked.

"I don't think it's that complicated. People who live in cities crave the natural world. And here it is. Beautiful. Wild. Wild, but contained. Thus, safe. And for sale."

I had stumbled yet again into the blur between art and commerce.

This time, there was no mistaking her sarcasm. "You

think I'm that calculating? That I make these pictures to satisfy a . . . commercial need?"

I hesitated, considering whether to cross the line, and decided. Oh, why not.

"Actually, I think you've made a different calculation. You choose these images because you don't want to reveal yourself."

"Jean Coin, woman of mystery?"

"If you don't want to put your emotions into your pictures, you have to find another way to reach people. You smartly chose distance. It's a powerful position."

I was afraid she'd slap me or storm off, but this seemed to please her.

"You could be a critic," she said.

"I appreciate the candor."

"That's only sort of a compliment."

Some people recognized Jean Coin and came over. Gears shifted.

"Well. A pleasure. Not that it matters—I'm David Greenfield."

"Got a card?"

"Sure." I produced one. "You?"

We traded the Japanese way, bowing slightly.

I thought I'd never see her again.

CHAPTER 4

I skipped the twentieth reunion of my class at Columbia Law because I'm just not nostalgic. Now I only go uptown when I'm asked to lecture. Every time, memories flash. Not the pain of torts and the Saturday nights in the library or the struggle to make law review. Only the pleasant memories: the ritual purchase of a Shetland sweater in the fall, plotting to separate Blair from her rich B-school boyfriend, Blair wearing my sweater as we talk over late-night coffee.

Barnard is as foreign to me now as it was when I was in law school. But Blair was—for the first time—leading a First-Year Class symposium. At dinner, when she summarized *The Wilder Shores of Love*, she made its profiles of four nineteenth-century English women come alive. They weren't head-in-the-stars dreamers; they were "realists of romance" who correctly understood that the epic lives they wanted weren't available in England's rigid social structure, so they fled to Algeria, Turkey, and Arabia. There they found men, adventure, and what they described as freedom.

When she talked about the book, my attendance felt compulsory.

Blair wasn't pleased.

"You'll be the only man," she said.

"Don't Columbia guys show up with their girlfriends?"

A sigh.

"And others come to meet the new girls?"

"Such things have been known to happen," she said.

"Essentially it's like a kegger with a brainiac overlay."

"Do you not understand that this is the most selective college for women in the country?"

"I do," I said. "And I get that this will be a hot ticket—in every sense of *hot*. And in that stew of ideas and nice-to-meet-yous, no one will notice the old duffer in the back row."

"You'll make me nervous."

"Maybe I'll come, maybe I won't—you'll have no idea if I'm there."

I wore a work shirt and jeans and sat in the back row near a gaggle of frat boys who'd come to scope out the new prey. I was noticed by a few Barnard students, who looked askance—what legit reason did an old guy who wasn't a professor have for being here?—until I held up my hand, patted my wedding band, and pointed to Blair.

"Context is key," Blair was saying. "You have to remember what England was like in the nineteenth century. In the upper class, marriage was a property deal, a merger of social equals. Women were expected to be faithful to the man they married, and they could be ruined if they were caught having an affair. But that wasn't the whole story, not nearly—at any house party at a country estate, guests were popping in and out of each other's bedrooms all weekend. These women rejected that hypocrisy. To them, love mattered."

"It still does," a young woman called out.

"But not as a first priority," another shouted.

"What is your first priority?" Blair asked.

"Paying off my student loan," a student said, to applause and laughter.

"Getting a job at Goldman," another said.

"Isn't that the same thing?" Blair asked.

The quickness of Blair's response took the students by surprise, and there was some laughter.

"I'm not joking," Blair said. "Seventeen percent of Columbia Business School graduates get hired at McKinsey, and eight percent get hired at Goldman, and the average starting salary at those shops is well over a hundred thousand. So your student loan may not be your first priority for long."

Blair paused.

I knew what she was doing: pretending to think. She knew what she would say next as surely as she knew, as far back as last week, she'd wear a thin cashmere sweater, a blazer, gray flannel pants, and no jewelry to this gathering.

"I get that you want professional opportunity and personal success," Blair said. "What I'm not getting is why your focus is so single-minded. What do you see yourselves doing at night?"

"Working late," a student said.

"The gym," another said.

The first student corrected herself. "Working late and hooking up."

"What's your number?" a Columbia kid shouted, prompting laughter and applause.

"Really?" Blair asked when the room quieted. "That's it?"

No one had more suggestions.

"Jane Digby wrote to one of her lovers: 'Being loved is to me as the air that I breathe.' I grant you, very mushy. But did anyone identify with her?"

Silence.

"*Agree* with her?"

Silence.

"*Like* her?"

A young woman stood, notebook in hand. "In 1799, Jane Digby's father seized a Spanish treasure ship. His share of the gold established the family fortune. So Jane, with no need to marry for money or earn a living, had the luxury of putting love first."

"They were all rich," the student next to her called out, "and all obsessed with men."

"I want their numbers too," the comedian from Columbia shouted, and, again, the room gave him the approval he craved.

Blair ignored the disruption.

"The author wasn't rich," she said. "Early in her career, she was supporting her parents."

"Doesn't matter." The student with the notebook opened her copy of *The Wilder Shades of Love*. "She aspired. Look at what she wrote: 'Admiration and love are the best beauty treatments.' The whole book is shot through with this stuff. It's totally male-centric."

"Isabelle Eberhardt dressed like a man and used a man's name," Blair countered. "And she married a soldier—how aspirational is that?"

Now it was a Barnard student who interjected: "She married a *man*."

There was no mistaking the derision in that student's voice. Blair looked at her watch.

"Let me reframe the issue, okay? We asked you to read this book because it was about women who shattered expectations. Out of the box? They kicked a hole in it and ran for daylight. Glass ceiling? They didn't look up; they looked inward. Career path? None. They were on what you might call"—a small private smile—"a journey. And that's the implicit question of this assignment: What's *your* journey? How long is its arc? How high? In your wildest dreams, how aspirational are you? I'm not hearing that yet."

Silence. This was one of those moments when everyone has an answer—who doesn't have a dream? —but no one wants to speak first.

A voice emerged from the middle of the room: "You start."

"Fair enough," Blair said. The slightest pause. "I'm married. I have a child. And I spend my days here with you. Freud said, 'Work and love.' Well, I'm with him. That's what I've got. That's what I cherish. I'm not saying you can have it all, because I don't and I know I can't, and I think that's the wrong conversation. But finding work worth doing and having people in your life worth doing it for . . . doing the best you can every day . . . that feels honorable to me."

These were not new ideas to these young women.

They were, in the main, their mothers' ideas. They were ideas their mothers had passed on to them. They had come to Barnard to reject these ideas, to find better ones, and what they were being told, by a woman they wanted to like and respect, was that these ideas were as good as it gets.

Unhappiness washed over the room.

Then, as Blair hoped, they began to say what they felt.

CHAPTER 5

If I didn't know she wanted half of her husband's frequent flyer miles, I might have thought Nancy Robb Russakof was irresistible. Eyes as gray as Nantucket fog. Bare, tanned legs. Black linen shirtwaist.

She wore an unidentifiable perfume that suggested the lavender fields and cypress trees of Provence, but whatever it was, her real scent was money—massive money. We had many clients like her. Their teeth were whitened, their toes and nails were glossy as Bentleys, their bodies were so kneaded and massaged that Kobe beef would be jealous.

Mrs. Russakof was entitled, but she was also nervous. I could tell because she stood in the doorway of my office, the heel of one ballet flat raised like a deer poised to pivot and flee at the slightest sign of danger.

Pleasantries were exchanged. I filled two heavy crystal glasses with gourmet water. To little effect. I only keep one picture in my office—of Blair and our daughter, taken when Ann was ten; they're walking hand in hand on a beach, love radiating from them in the golden late afternoon—and the absence of framed degrees or signed photos from grateful celebrities compounded Mrs. Russakof's discomfort. I let her stew. She wanted Victoria, not me. All attempts to charm her would be unavailing.

She spoke first. "Did Victoria brief you?"

"Yes. The general idea was short-man syndrome."

"He's tall when he stands on his wallet."

"Those weren't her words, but—"

"They're key. He's not going to make this easy."

"The spouse writing the checks rarely does."

"Then Victoria didn't really brief you." She leaned forward, resentment streaming off her. "Billy started out as a bond trader for Milken and left before Boesky fooled the government into thinking Mike was Mr. Big. He took his loot, bought a company, flipped it, and became a player. He hit Eastern Europe just behind Soros, made the Forbes list, married me, and decided we should be the next power couple in women's wear. See where I'm going, Mr. Greenfield? He's always a step ahead. And widely hated for it."

"Widely?"

"You don't know the joke about him? You have Osama bin Laden, Adolf Hitler, and Billy Russakof in a room. And you have a gun. But you only have two bullets. Who do you shoot?"

"No idea."

"Billy Russakof—twice."

"Oh. Why do you want to end the marriage now?"

"A few months ago, instead of working late or going out with his traders at night or screwing an assistant, Billy began coming home for dinner."

"What did this suggest to you?"

"That I needed to go to the clue store. Really. I had no idea."

"You might have taken that as a fresh commitment to the marriage. Why didn't you?"

"Because all he talks about are his trades. The bid. The ask. The number of shares. His reasoning. Their reasoning. It was excruciating. I started drinking glass after glass of water just so I could leave the table and pee."

"He's trying to drive you crazy."

"For starters, yes."

"He knows you're here?"

"Billy's not above hiding a GPS in my bag."

Another woman might have said it was a Birkin, which it was, selling for $20,000, at least. She didn't go there. Points for her.

"Mrs. Russakof, are you having an affair?"

She ignored the question, produced a brown envelope, and set it on my desk. She knew her business—it was sealed and signed on the flap, with clear tape over the signature.

"Put this in your safe," she said. "How soon can we start?"

I pushed an extension on the phone. "If you have a few minutes . . ."

This impressed her. "You have a forensic accountant on staff?"

"Not exactly an accountant. But definitely an expert. He's been with Victoria for a long time. Before he comes in, two things you should know: He's not a mute, just very silent, and he prefers not to use his name. You'll know him as Reboot."

"Reboot?"

"He's a master of the art of getting—and forgetting. Swiss bank records, mistresses, whatever we need. All very discreet."

She nodded. With the matrimonial business with me over, she took up some personal business.

"Just so we're clear, Mr. Greenfield," she said, "I don't sleep with married men."

"I don't either," I replied.

A soft, timely knock on the door. Reboot appeared. He was exactly as described: not memorable.

I made introductions. Reboot nodded. Nancy Russakof seemed slightly intimidated. And as she began to outline her husband's enterprise, I dared to think maybe we'd hear no more of air miles.

Then I had other thoughts: tanned legs, gray eyes, and lavender perfume.

CHAPTER 6

When Jean Coin called to ask if we could meet—"It's not urgent but as soon as possible, outside the office"—I took that to mean she wanted maximum privacy. Once I got over my surprise and set aside my curiosity, I knew where to have this conversation: the café at the model boat pond in Central Park, a cheery stage set where rich kids and their fathers sail small, radio-controlled boats. On weekends, it's mobbed. On a school day in September, the tables would be empty.

My office was six blocks away. Jean Coin's loft was in Tribeca. Of course she arrived first.

She was standing with her back to me, a foot on a chair, retying a shoelace. White shirt, faded jeans, sneakers. Her all-purpose uniform.

"Ms. Coin?"

She turned.

"Sorry to be late," I said. "Weepy client."

"If you're not early, you're late," she said, but then I got a smile I didn't expect and a quick, awkward kiss on the cheek I expected even less.

At the gallery, her gaze had been so powerful and our conversation so intense that I didn't really notice much else. I did now. She had a look much prized in our city. Memorable cheekbones. Legs so thin it looked as if the bones could snap at any time. Breasts, and not small ones.

I felt . . . stirrings.

She claimed the chair with her back to the pond. Her view: a stone wall, the tops of buses, the trunks of trees, and, through the foliage, a sliver of limestone apartment buildings on Fifth Avenue, which is to say she had no view at all. I understood her choice when I took the chair that looked into the park—the better view. Jean was a picture waiting to be taken, the woman in the center of the frame with stripes of water and lawn behind her.

On the table sat two bottles of Evian and two sandwiches precisely wrapped in paper napkins.

"Ham and brie, with honey mustard," she said. "Okay?"

"Salami and cheddar would have been fine. But thanks."

Multitasking seemed unwise. I didn't unwrap my sandwich.

"Hypothetically," she said as she opened her bottle of water, "what makes a client weepy?"

"Hypothetically . . . he's due in court next month, and he just fired his fourth lawyer. But even as he's pleading poverty, he bought a ranch in"—professional discretion made me pause and go vague—"some Rocky Mountain state. With separate pilot's quarters. Don't you love that phrase?"

"I don't understand. What are pilot's quarters . . . hypothetically?"

Did Jean Coin giggle? No. But close.

"Hypothetically," I began—now her laugh was full-throated, and I could almost see her knocking back shots of bourbon in a bar a half hour before closing—"pilot's quarters means an apartment over the garage for the pilot of your private jet."

"The pilot can't stay in a motel?"

"Not the pilot of a CEO's G5. Not in an unnamed mountain state resort."

"Will the husband win?"

"Hypothetically . . . no. But my weeper and I will sweat to earn every dollar. And then we'll have to wait for it. That's how these guys operate."

"If you had him for a client . . ."

"Men like that," I said, "are why my partner and I prefer to represent the wives."

"This is so much more interesting than photography," Jean said. "If you can talk about it . . . what's the best present a client has ever given you?"

"Gratitude. And tears. Good tears."

"No 'now that I'm not your client, maybe we could . . .'?"

"Hypothetically, no. And, in fact, no. A better question would be: What's the best present you ever got from a client's ex-husband?"

"That happened?"

"Once. Two bottles of '78 Petrus . . . with a card that said *thank you*."

"He must have been very relieved to be rid of her."

"No doubt. But I think he was sending me a message: 'You missed the twenty million dollars I stashed offshore.'"

Jean's reaction was pretty much nothing, and I began to suspect that she was more interested in running a line of questions than hearing the answers. I don't mind sharing war stories—it's one of the perks of the profession. Doing it at a party is one thing, but doing it for a woman who has summoned you from your office in midday? Enjoyable at first, just because it was Jean Coin, but getting old fast.

"Ms. Coin . . ."

"One more, okay?"

"One."

"What was the meanest thing a husband ever did to his wife?"

"So many to choose from. But this is a classic. . . . She put him through med school. He became successful. Just before their anniversary, he told her, 'Go to Bergdorf's and try on fur coats.' She did. Left him a note about the coat she liked and the woman who'd helped her. The anniversary came and went. Nothing. She mustered some courage and asked what had gone wrong. 'Oh, trying on the coat—that was your present,' he said. And yet she stayed married to him for five more years."

She looked down at her sandwich, clearly uneasy. Seconds ticked by; minutes might follow. "What's the most amazing thing a client ever told you?" This was blurted out. As if she were stalling. Why?

"That's a second question."

"Please."

This took no effort. I think about this woman all the time.

"I represented a woman who would go, once a month, to a hotel, where three or four guys were waiting. She'd do them all, one after another. And then she'd go home to her husband. I asked her why she did it, why she liked it. 'Because it's just . . . filthy,' she said, and the look on her face when she said that last word . . . it was rapture."

"*Rapture*," she said. "Is that not the most beautiful word in the English language?"

I could have suggested others: *again* and *more*. But that story about the client in the hotel room was the end of the pleasantries for me. I wanted Jean to state her business.

"Did you want to see me about a . . . matrimonial issue, Ms. Coin?"

"Oh, I'm not married, counselor," she said. "This is . . . social."

Again she descended into silence, jaw clenched. At last she said, "Promise me you won't laugh."

"Cross my heart."

She took several calming breaths but was no calmer for them.

In a rush: "I'm leaving the city for six months at Thanksgiving, and I'd like to have a lover until then, and I'd like you . . ."

She couldn't make it to the end. But she was looking right at me, and her eyes said it all.

"I could not possibly be more surprised," I said.

"Surprised—and flattered?"

"I may get to *flattered*. Right now, I'm stuck on *surprised*."

Not what she hoped to hear.

"I'm sorry," she said. "I *can* do foreplay, but not at the beginning."

"Funny, that's when it's usually done."

I meant a light tone, but I missed. Why the sarcasm? Because although I'm a good man, I am, in the end, just a man. Monogamy-challenged. Eternally. I know this—early in my marriage, there was some nasty trouble on just this issue—so I walk the line. I don't hide my wedding ring or maneuver conversations with married women in the direction of lies about my "open marriage" or initiate any strategy that could lead to a woman's bed without that seeming to be my idea. Blair says I'm a flirt, but I don't think women are confused—my idea of flirting is more like banter.

I've never directly propositioned anyone.

A woman bluntly propositioning *me*? It's never happened. But here was Jean Coin, shoving temptation in my face. Many men would be thrilled. And maybe I would be, if I allowed myself to admit it.

So I admitted it.

Reality check—my defenses had been breached. I'd almost forgotten the signals, but here they were: dry mouth, pounding pulse, and a surge of blood. Another minute and I'd pull her to me and lock mouths.

"I need to be elsewhere," I said.

An obvious lie but apparently obvious only to me.

"You're shocked."

"It's more like . . . I feel that I should respond in . . . oh . . . French. Or Swedish."

Such bullshit. And worse—cowardly. Sophisticated New York lawyer David Greenfield would do battle for a woman, but he'd do anything to avoid confronting her.

Jean missed my evasion. I'd rejected her; anything else was just noise. And the rejection grated.

"You really ought to get out more," she said.

No mistaking her edge.

"Yeah? Where?" I asked, with edge of my own.

"Any bar. Any city. Any day of the week. It's as American as the NRA—people hit on each other."

"No, men hit on women."

"Boy, you are weak on the facts."

Nasty. Condescending. I went into my default: Play the lawyer, and grill the witness.

"The facts are subtext. I'm hung up on the main point, like why me?"

"In your business, when you meet someone, do you ever get a . . . feeling?"

"All the time," I said, evenly. "But I never act on first impressions."

Now Jean looked completely defeated. When she spoke, she mumbled.

"I sensed a restlessness . . . I felt a possibility . . . I hoped you'd find me attractive. I hoped—"

"Jean, I have a wife."

"All the good men do."

"Find another one. My marriage doesn't work that way."

"How does it work?"

My God, she was relentless. Somewhere this was a virtue.

"Actually, I don't think you're entitled to an answer."

"You only regret what you say no to," she said.

I could hear her hurt and see her disappointment, but there was no civil way to end this. I got up and walked away, not looking back.

CHAPTER 7

For eighteen years, we rarely went out on Saturday night. Friends might come over. Or Ann would have a sleepover, and we'd have half a dozen girls chattering in the next room till all hours. Or, in recent years, Ann and her boyfriend of the season would join us for dinner before they went out to wherever it is that kids go.

But with Ann off to college, we were starting fresh. We had to. Our married friends were our age, but they seemed a generation younger. They'd waited until thirty to marry, thirty-five to have kids; when we were taking Ann on the college tour, they were sweating acceptance to kindergarten.

And now, at forty-six, we were empty nesters. Impossible to accept. Just the two of us? For decades and decades? How crazy was that?

But okay. Change, the law of life. Saturday now meant sushi in the neighborhood followed by a movie.

Blair had gone to snag seats, so I was the one in the popcorn line. Just ahead of me was a woman in her early thirties. It was a warm night, and she was wearing a sleeveless blouse with no sweater, tight black jeans, and black boots.

Standing behind her, I couldn't help but notice that her bra was too tight; in back of the armholes, it forced tabs of flesh into public view. Worse, it announced that there was no one in her life who saw her from behind before she went out.

The line was moving slowly. There were twenty people ahead of us. She wasn't checking her phone. On weekends, I never do. So it was boredom or chat.

"This is like being in a bank line," I said.

"I wouldn't know. I'm unemployed."

"Oh. Who did you used to be?"

"HR for an investment bank—the first to go. You?"

"Lawyer."

"Wall Street?"

"Matrimonial. What are you seeing?"

"The vampire movie."

"Aren't you a little old for that?"

"My friends said that. So I'm here by myself."

We were moving steadily along, almost at the front of the line.

"I don't get it," I said. "What's the attraction of having a guy suck your blood?"

"It's not the blood. It's the neck."

A clerk called out: "Next."

"Women also like to have their necks *licked*," she said, and she gave me a fifty-watt smile as she walked away.

How do you read an encounter like that?

As a New York moment: two people, a brisk exchange, happens all the time, on to the next.

Or—and the thought sent my pulse redlining—this unemployed woman who used to work in HR at an investment bank was alone and up for anything on a warm Saturday night in mid-September.

CHAPTER 8

I don't remember his name, and I doubt his book outlived him, but I sometimes think of a man who's been dead for more than a century. He was French. Titled. Rich in a time when that meant going out four nights a week. It took him only minutes to put on a dinner jacket; his wife required an hour to dress. Rather than seethe, he decided to write a novel while he waited for her to appear. In less than a year, he'd finished it.

My situation is just the reverse. *After* a night out, I'm waiting for my wife to undress. To wash the day away. And then put on an outfit only I'll see.

I'm quick—I shower between the drops, Blair says—so I go first.

Then, while Blair disappears, I have tasks.

I have performed them two or three nights a week—for years.

They never get old.

Pour two shots of tequila or single malt and two glasses of water. Roll a thin joint. Light a candle. Choose music that can take us elsewhere.

Sometimes I hear Blair singing. Saturday night she was silent. Until, through the bathroom door, she announced what she'd been thinking about.

"That line in the movie—do you think that's true?"

"Which one?" I asked, though I knew the line she meant.

The door opened. Blair was wearing a thick white terrycloth robe. And spiked heels. I hoped for a short conversation.

She quoted: "Making love to your wife is like striking out the pitcher."

"You were offended?"

"You weren't?"

"Right after he said that, she slugged him—and the audience laughed."

"First they laughed at his line," she said.

"But she got the last laugh."

I handed Blair a shot glass. She drained it and then took the second glass—my glass—and knocked it back.

"Something for him, something for her," she pointed out. "They had it every which way."

"It worked," I said. "We're talking about it now. And you know . . ." I lit the joint and handed it to her. "It's not exactly our problem."

There are so many ways to start. Fingers resting on a pulsing vein on the wrist. A whisper, a warm breath in the ear. A hand between the legs, gently cupping.

Or the direct approach. Like Blair loosening her robe, revealing a black thong and a low-cut black bra that made her breasts look wonderfully swollen.

The thong. Is it not the greatest advance in fashion since the miniskirt? Never fails to delight. It banishes all other fantasies. It commands: This is where you'll focus.

A strong man could resist a thong. I am not that man.

A thong does not necessarily lead to hot, dirty frenzy, but for Blair and me, it often does: grabbing, squeezing, probing, shrieks and shouts, spontaneous tears, ecstatic merging, a climax that feels as if it's accompanied by a two-by-four to the back of the neck and a vacuuming of every cell in the body, leaving us cleansed and revived in the few seconds before we fall asleep like truckers.

Or it's the opposite: a slow-motion meditation on a square inch, a single sensation, a frozen gesture, time slowing, an almost imperceptibly spreading heat, a silent explosion, and a gentle emptying, like the tide rushing out.

So it was on Saturday night. Or so it was for Blair on Saturday night. This wasn't sex for her; it was making love—smooth and flowing and life enhancing. And why not? Her daughter was off at an elite college. Her husband was satisfied by his work, committed to his family, faithful to his wife. On her desk were sharpened pencils, in her closet new skirts, in her heart a hope for better that marked the start of every school year for her. No country home, no offshore accounts, no Manolos, but good sheets on the bed, wholesome food in the cupboard, an orderly household, a cool breeze from the park—in an unsteady, corrupt world, this was happiness of a high order.

I felt all that and responded to it, but the woman in the refreshment line at the movies had unsettled me—I couldn't keep my focus on Blair.

I thought of women from my distant past, women I cherished when sex was new and I thought that women were my real teachers and my education was best conducted in bed. The long lost girlfriend with lovely, full breasts, breasts so big she could hold them up and lick her nipples. The college girl, a friend of a friend, who stayed with me for a few days when I was in law school and who came into the kitchen one morning as I was brewing coffee, opened her towel, and made me late for class. The articles editor of the law review, who showed up with a peacock feather, and the visitor from Toronto who liked it standing on the roof at midnight when it was just starting to snow and the city was silent.

In between, my head flashed images of Blair, but not the Blair who was in bed with me. Blair half-naked at midnight in the service elevator of a cheap Paris hotel, Blair in the backseat of a rented car, Blair whispering about doing it with a man whose face she never sees. Hot images, heart-stopping memories.

Then I thought of a more recent Blair: Blair at forty. For that birthday, she let me make a video of her. Just her, naked, in the bedroom—she put on a show. When it was over and she lay quivering, I turned the camera off and gave it to her. She put it away. I've never seen it since. She may have destroyed it.

It was a total surprise when I conjured Jean Coin, in an unbuttoned white shirt, her jeans falling to her ankles, eyes wide open, lips moistened, hands reaching toward me, and I did that thing I can honestly say I've never done before—I had my orgasm thinking of a woman who was not my wife.

CHAPTER 9

On Monday, I called Jean Coin.

I didn't think I would, but I did.

Blair and I had discussed this moment—what to do when someone's tempted to stray—and we'd developed an adultery killer, a solution so simple there could be no possibility of confusion.

This wasn't a theoretical, what-if conversation.

There was some history.

Two years into our marriage, with our daughter still in diapers, I had an affair. I wasn't overwhelmed by young fatherhood or turned off by a lactating wife. I had a "deeper" rationale—I felt it was crucial not to commit completely to any relationship; I thought it was soul-saving to keep a sliver of me for me. And, inevitably, I met a young, newly married lawyer at a conference who felt the same way. Hours after we met, we were having incendiary, bounce-off-the-walls sex.

I got caught because I was a fool. My lover and I collected the small bars of gourmet soap you get in better hotels. To use that soap at home produced a secret smile in the morning. And to see that soap next to the grocery-store brand that Blair used gave me a sense of abundance.

Yes, I was quite the sophisticate.

In a matter of months, Blair figured out something was going on. Holy hell followed and weeks of no sex, a punishment that punished us both. Then something surprising: a fresh idea, reality-based, looking a lot more like wisdom than the dull affirmations you find in the how-to-be-married guides.

What I proposed was this: If you're tempted to stray—if you find yourself moving beyond an innocent flirt—you've got to stop and tell that person: "I have a partner who is the dearest person in the world to me. Cheating may be okay for others, but it's not okay for me, not okay for us. So I can't do this alone." And then ask: "May I bring you home?"

Our theory—Blair immediately saw the logic, so I considered it *our* theory—is that any couple is a group of two. So is an affair. It's just a different person who's on the outside. But if you expand the circle, nobody's left out. An infatuation that might have become marriage threatening is reduced to . . . an episode. A couple can then grow old together without hypocrisy or deception.

But here I was, considering a solo hookup with Jean Coin once a week for five or six weeks, a complete violation of my understanding with Blair. Not a misdemeanor—a felony.

Why was I about to do it?

When you're justifying yourself, you always have answers:

I've been so good for so long, I'm owed.

My wife knows me, every last corner; I know her, in every possible way; we're bonded. And while that's thrilling, it's also diminishing—I've become nothing more than half of a couple.

I've been feeling a pressure that needs relief, a pressure my wife can't tap. I wear sunglasses even on cloudy days so I can check out the breasts of women walking my way. I follow any woman with an attractive ass, just to watch. If I don't do something to relieve the pressure, I'll start locking my office door, watching porn on my computer, and . . .

I'm not as hot for my partner as I used to be. I crave someone new. And I just happen to know who . . .

Those reasons are all the same reason, which is the punch line of this joke: Two guys walk into a restaurant. At a table, alone, clearly waiting for someone, is the most beautiful woman in the world. One of the men says, "Somewhere there's a guy who's sick of fucking her."

I wasn't sick of Blair. I didn't crave a new thrill. I didn't feel that years of fidelity entitled me to a no-fault affair. I had success in my work and stability in my home and, most of all, I loved Blair even more than I did on our wedding day—I envied my own life.

So why get involved with Jean Coin?

I told myself that Jean was a dream lover—a nomad in her work, a hermit in New York. A walking secret and almost certain to remain that way. Somewhere inside, there was a lonely, vulnerable person, but a short-term lover would never have to meet her. The boundaries of the relationship were the four corners of a bed. Once a week. For six weeks. Then gone, and good-bye. As I say, a dream.

This isn't an explanation, and, looking back, I can't re-create one. The best I can do: Something was wrong with me. I couldn't name it. I didn't want to think about it. But instead of doing nothing, instead of letting my distress pass, I took a step forward.

* * *

She answered on the first ring, as if she knew I'd call, and soon.

"Second thoughts, counselor?"

I was a high school debater, a sometime actor in college, and a star of moot court in law school. But when I opened my mouth, I might as well have been fourteen.

"As a matter of fact . . ." I said, then went silent.

"Would this be easier in person?" she asked.

"Maybe."

Without irony: "Our place?"

I looked at my calendar.

"Give me an hour."

The afternoon shadows darkened the green of the park and brightened the sparkle of the boat pond. The walks were pebbled with horse chestnuts. Thanksgiving seemed like next week. I felt an irrational urgency.

Jean was just back from some beach. Her hair was lighter and her tan deeper; her perfume was sunscreen. Today she was beautiful in the way of an athlete. Her health and vitality were like a force field.

"I hated how it ended last time," she said. "Whatever happens between us, I'm glad we're seeing each other."

Generous. And why not? Last week she was the one with her hand out. Today I was—well, I was the suitor, wasn't I? I mean, I was the one who called.

"This is beyond awkward," I said.

"Why?"

"I know how this is done. I've read books, my clients tell me stories. And . . . obviously . . . but . . ."

"Let's walk," she said. She reached for my arm, hesitated. "Is this okay?"

"Yes."

On any other day, I would have said no. It isn't. Because anyone encountering us with Jean's hand resting on my arm as we walked deeper into the park would have thought: What a nice couple.

And if anyone who encountered us happened to know me, the next thought would have been: That's no couple; that's David and his lover.

But I didn't care.

"I'm pleased about this," Jean said.

"You've done this before," I said. "So enlighten me. Is it really this . . . clinical? Is it just about sex?"

Jean laughed. "You're complaining?"

Rueful me. "I know it sounds like I just got off the bus from the farm. But—"

"Don't worry," Jean said. "We'll find some affection."

"Let's seal this," I said. "Kiss me."

Jean turned to me. "All yours," she said.

"For six weeks."

"Shhh," she said, and pressed her lips to mine.

The only woman I'd kissed on the mouth since Bill Clinton was president was my wife, so I stood apart from Jean, not moving closer, connected to her only by the kiss. It felt weird, kissing and yet not holding each other, but she allowed it. Then she rested a hand on my cheek, and I was lost.

I pulled her close and kissed harder. Her heart was beating almost frighteningly fast. She slipped a hand inside my suit jacket, clutching the back of my shirt, and thrust a leg between mine, as if daring me to rub myself to orgasm against her.

Strangeness. The feeling that I wasn't quite in my body, that I was an onlooker, and it was all interesting but also random, as if I might choose to change a channel and watch something else. Not that there was anything more compelling.

And then a sudden dizziness, a burst of brain scatter and spinning, leaves and clouds and sky rushing at me. I pulled back, reached out for something solid, found nothing, and grabbed Jean by both shoulders.

I heard a distant voice: "David?"

Head down. Slow, deep breaths. Like a diver, coming slowly

to the surface, I felt bubbles in my head, rising and bursting, leaving a blessed silence behind. Clarity slowly regained.

Jean, visibly concerned: "Okay?"

"Let's sit."

The bench was painted dark green, with a brass plaque, shiny, of recent vintage. Jean's white shirt gleamed. The day was saturated with color. Beauty everywhere.

"Sorry if I scared you."

"This has happened before?"

"No."

"I've never thought to ask someone to take a physical before we went to bed."

"Well, that was a lightning bolt of a kiss," I said.

"In both directions." A girlish smile. "Again?"

I rested my hands on Jean's arms. She thought we were about to kiss and closed her eyes. But I was looking at her as if seeing her for the first time. I registered her intelligence, her independence, her self-awareness, her appetite for experience, and, far from least, her beauty.

Nothing I saw told me to turn back.

Then I flashed on Blair. At home. A domestic scene, a nothing moment: taking coffee cups out of the dishwasher and putting them away. In her head was something like peace.

It's been so long since I've done this, it's entirely possible I'd suck at it. Shower before leaving Jean's loft, arrive home with wet hair. Turn curt and moody. Announce the affair without announcing it. Wreck everything.

Jean, unkissed and confused, opened her eyes.

"I could tell you a story—but I'll cut to the end."

I paused. I'd never said these words before. I couldn't quite believe I was about to say them now. "I can't have an affair with you. I can take you home."

"Home . . . to your wife?"

"Yes."

"A threesome?"

I made an attempt at humor. "Call it a ménage à trois."

Wicked smile. "Once a week, for six weeks?"

"Once. Just once."

"Isn't a threesome just a twosome with one person watching?"

"For some people."

"But not you," she said.

"I wouldn't know."

Jean was amused. "You've read a book, seen a movie . . ."

"I've had clients try it," I said.

"To 'save the marriage,' yes?"

"Yes."

"And they're all divorced now, aren't they?"

"Yes."

"But you're suggesting it anyway."

"Not because it's my preference."

"Why not? Isn't the threesome every man's favorite fantasy?"

"So they say."

"Incredibly appealing, isn't it? Big tits. Shaved pussies. And after, an ice cream sundae with whipped cream and a cherry."

"It wouldn't be like that," I said. "We're not like that."

"What are 'we' like?"

"We're . . ." I wanted just the right word, but one was way too few. "We're . . . okay."

"How hot is 'okay'?"

"Not for me to say."

A curator's look of appraisal. The briefest thought.

"Okay," she said. "Take me home."

CHAPTER 10

I could have talked to Blair about Jean Coin at home, but I was on a high. Jean was good news. I wanted to share it in a place where the exalted go to celebrate.

I know who I am in the great chain of being: a servant of Manhattan's ruling class. Not a bold-faced name. Not a divorce lawyer on the speed dial of talk-show bookers. Definitely not someone who can get a table at one of the city's shrines to celebrity chefs.

If I called to make a reservation at a three- or four-star restaurant, I'd almost surely be told that we could be squeezed in a month from now at five thirty.

But in September, there's an exception.

If you want a reservation anywhere in New York on the night of Yom Kippur, you're in.

On that holiest of nights, Jews are in synagogues, fasting and praying. Or at home, guiltily eating Chinese takeout. But they're definitely not eating Bresse chicken in a three-star restaurant. So at the upper end of fine dining, many of the regular patrons are otherwise engaged—and when you call, you get decent treatment.

I called Per Se, the most expensive restaurant in the city. *What time is best for you, Mr. Greenfield? Eight o'clock? Looking forward.*

I told Blair we were going out, that the destination was swellegant and to dress accordingly. I didn't tell her where we were going—we'd done this before, making plans without telling the other, presenting an evening as a surprise. But when the cab stopped at the Time Warner Center, Blair was quizzical. Why the black dress, pearls, and slingbacks if we were bound for Whole Foods or Barnes & Noble?

There are several restaurants on the fourth floor. Blair saw the steakhouse first and wasn't thrilled; fifty dollars worth of beef would have her computing how many gallons of water it takes to produce a pound of meat. Actually, it wouldn't. She knows, and I've heard the lecture: thirty-seven gallons.

Then she saw Per Se.

"David . . ."

I opened the door and held it for her. She had no choice. She stepped inside.

A few heads turned. One was that of Nancy Robb Russakof, at a table with a man who could only be her husband. She nodded, almost imperceptibly. Her husband had his back to me and was chatting with the sommelier; he missed the exchange.

Seated, we reached for our napkins. They were so impossibly soft that Blair held hers to her cheek.

Blair took my hand. "This will cost . . ."

"Don't look right now, but the blonde in a gray dress . . ."

Only Blair's eyes moved.

"With the trillion-dollar necklace?"

"My new client. With her soon-to-be-former husband— consider dinner on him."

When Blair sees wealth, she wonders what crime was committed to get it. She looked around the room and saw who was in the night's cast—a random assortment of Wall Street chieftains, media executives, and unrecognizable foodies—and any small pleasure she felt evaporated.

"Why are we here?" Blair asked.

"There are only sixteen tables," I said. "You can have an intimate conversation and not be overheard."

Stupid line. It bathed Blair in concern.

"What's the topic, David?"

"Nothing bad."

"Just being here feels bad."

"We'll never come back."

A waiter materialized. Blair looked up and smiled.

"In that case," she said, "we would like champagne."

The meal began with Per Se's signature offering: Northern California white sturgeon caviar atop a half dozen Island Creek oysters from Massachusetts resting on a bed of tapioca in a Limoges bowl. With it, we drank a Sémillon that added velvet to the brine, salt, and custard.

Blair didn't want the caviar. And in a better world, I'd be marching alongside her in protest against luxury and excess. But she ate it—all of it. She was right to. This was a voluptuous sensation. After, we sat in stunned silence.

Blair broke it, as I knew she would.

"So what's the secret?"

"I've had an . . . offer."

Victoria is like family to Blair. Her reaction was immediate. "You can't leave V! You can't!"

"Not a professional offer."

Blair looked confused. What other kind was there?

"A personal offer. An invitation." I paused. "More like a proposition."

"Oh," she said, with considerable relief. "Who?"

"Jean Coin."

The name was lost on Blair.

"A photographer. Arty. Successful. I went to the opening of her show. She was there. We talked. A few days later, she told me she was going away at Thanksgiving and wanted me to be her lover until then."

"What did you tell her?"

"That I couldn't be her lover without you being there."

Was Blair pleased? Appalled? I couldn't tell.

At last: "So what did she say?"

"She'd like to meet you."

"Well, then." A long breath followed. "After all these years of talk . . . here it is."

"What do you think?"

"I'm now thinking I'd be more comfortable if we hired someone. If we met at a hotel, made up names. In a few hours she'd be gone, and it would be like it never happened. A private experience guaranteed to remain private—why is this photographer woman better than that?"

"Hiring someone feels . . . cold. Clinical. However she responds . . . it's fake."

"Yeah, but with someone in the arts, there's just enough in common that she could be a friend of a friend. Later, we might run into her."

"I've thought of that too," I said. "But it comes down to this. There are couples who go to clubs and drink enough to take someone home. And couples who read ads for escorts like they were shopping at Amazon. But we're not those people. If we're going to do this, it has to be with a . . . person."

Blair looked out at the park. "When you see the three of us together . . ."

"Got an hour?" I asked.

A reassuring laugh. "I'll take the short list."

Oh, I had a short one. And a long one, a much longer one, so extensive that it might make better sense as a Power-Point presentation. But what came to mind at that moment wasn't all the hot, thrilling ways I saw the three of us playing together; it was pride. In my wife. In our marriage. In our ability to have a conversation on a topic that would surely have the diners at the other tables red-faced and tongue-tied. In our very intelligent way of confronting the challenge of monogamy. And in our very smart solution, one that would make our marriage stronger.

"I see a lot of things," I said. "In the beginning, I see you and Jean just . . . kissing. I see your blouse . . ."

"Pretty tame," Blair said.

"It's our first time. Best to take it slow."

"You think I'm going to freak out? After all the vile scenarios you've poured into my ear?"

"Right," I said. "Those."

"We're going to see this woman . . ." Blair blanked on the name.

"Jean Coin."

"We're going to see Jean Coin once and do all those things?"

"Maybe just Column A."

"Is she . . ."

"Not quite as beautiful as you."

A nod. Then a mood shift. Blair looked down at the table as if she'd just been told she had a minute to cram for an unannounced final exam on the silver setting. I said nothing; one thing I've learned from interviewing clients is not to break a silence with a first draft of the answer I want. And with Blair, I wasn't sure what answer I wanted.

"I've been doing a lot of thinking since Ann left," Blair said. "And I've seen how . . . grooved our lives are. Mine, anyway. When she was in school, I was really tethered. Happily, basically. The child, the job, the marriage. Friends on the fringe, but this is New York; everybody understands that your friends are the only people you don't see. Now, with Ann gone, I'm thinking I should change . . . something. Get a hobby. Find a cause. But nothing comes to mind."

"So . . . this?"

"This, for openers. And not just this. I've been thinking, no matter what the question is, my first answer should be yes. I'm not going to be a fool. I'll reconsider everything, and if I change my mind, well, so be it. But at the start, I'm going to affirm. Everything. And if I do that, my life will change."

"For the better?" I asked. "Always for the better?"

"No idea," she said, and raised a glass. "To change!"

Many courses followed, all small. More wine than we're used to. The hour grew late. The moon filled the restaurant windows. And we were filled too, less by dinner than by a sense of contentment and expectation. We'd made a plan. We were stepping into the future, together.

CHAPTER 11

At any moment, at a very low emotional cost, I could permanently postpone my fantasy. I wasn't doing that. I was advancing the plan. But everything that was happening seemed to be in the hands of the gods. I had no power here—it was as if I were watching a movie about characters who just happened to have our names.

So, late on a weekday afternoon, Blair and I found ourselves in an empty art gallery. Blair looked at Jean's photographs while I stood at the reception desk, watching, a voyeur twice over—there was Blair, and there was Jean's work, her icebergs, her mountains and monuments making Blair seem small. Then, as Blair walked toward me, Jean's pictures receded, and I could focus just on my wife, her eyes shining with admiration for Jean's work.

As we walked home, I backpedaled: "Just to get it on the record, we don't have to do this."

"We're committed to nothing," Blair said. "First I need to meet Jean in a way that's not . . . awkward."

Coffee? Too banal.

A dinner party, with our friends never suspecting what was going on? Blair's best friend, Jared, who's mildly psychic, would have twigged that something was afoot, and Blair, who hates to lie, would have spilled the secret.

Or . . . but there was no other bright idea. So, after all, it was coffee.

What do you wear to a meeting with a woman who wants to sleep with you and your wife?

I don't usually shave on Sunday. But jeans, running shoes, and stubble didn't seem right for our coffee date with Jean Coin, so I tried on half a dozen shirts of varying degrees of informality before I surrendered to my off-duty uniform since college: a striped oxford shirt and khakis.

Blair cares about clothes and is smart about them, but she downplayed it and did that weekend thing where you dress well but not up: cotton sweater, jeans with a rip at the knee, a leather-and-silver bracelet, and moccasins. She looked beautiful. And pedigreed. And rich. But mostly, comfortable and self-confident—everything she wasn't quite feeling.

In a state of numb attractiveness we found ourselves walking across the park on a glorious Sunday afternoon in late September.

We'd arranged to meet Jean at Via Quadronno, an East Side coffee bar and restaurant that is the exact opposite of Starbucks. The entrance is almost impassably narrow, the coffee bar always crowded. In the small room in the back, shoppers from the designer stores on Madison and Italians too chic to be labeled tourists order paninis and salad. We like this place for the delicious sociology but even more for the barista, who makes the best cappuccino for miles.

We arrived early and waited outside, among the smokers and couples with dogs. A church bell tolled the hour. Jean strolled up, on time to the minute. In a pink shirt, suede jacket, and jeans with no rip in the knee, she looked quite at home in this zip code.

I touched Blair's hand, giving her a second of warning.

"Blair, this is—"

"Jean Coin," Jean said.

Was there a tremble in her voice? Was she nervous too?

Blair and Jean reached out to shake hands at the same

time. And laughed. Like they'd thought about this moment and had come to the same idea.

"David," Jean said.

She offered her cheek, which I dutifully kissed.

"Coffee?" Blair asked.

"It's too nice to be inside," Jean said. "Can we—"

"I'll get it," I said.

I could feel Blair stiffen at the prospect of being alone with Jean so soon.

Jean read the moment correctly. "Cappuccino?" she asked. We nodded, and she went into the restaurant.

"Decisive," Blair said.

I took that as approval.

As we walked into the park, Blair opened with a safe, correct move: "I loved the show."

I could have predicted Jean's response. "The last one was better."

And they were off.

"I can't see how," Blair said.

"Technical things. I'll get it right next time."

"In the pictures you'll take this winter?"

"Yes. In Timbuktu."

"What's there?"

"Shrines. And a mosque. A mosque with an incredible door."

"Incredible because . . ."

"It's been closed for six centuries. And tradition says it must stay closed until Judgment Day."

"It's never been photographed?"

"Not well. And that may not change—the Taliban's been making trouble in the area."

"What if you can't go?"

The first reference to the real business at hand.

"I promise you, by Thanksgiving I will be on another continent."

"What's Plan B?"

"The northern coast of Germany. For the beach houses. Like the Hamptons."

"Why not just go to Long Island?"

"The Hampton beaches are better protected. In Germany, if the ocean keeps rising, these houses will be underwater in twenty years. Shooting from a small boat at high tide, the pictures will look as if I took them just before the fatal waves hit."

"You're not going to sell those pictures as house portraits to the owners," I said.

"I didn't expect to," Jean said, and if I wasn't mistaken,

there was a touch of irritation in her voice, as if she'd heard me say all she ever wanted to hear about the commercial aspect of her work.

My stupid little comment broke the mood. Why had I interrupted? Feeling left out, perhaps? How like a man!

We reached the vine-covered terrace, a haven for chess players. At the one empty table, Jean sat across from us. Hard not to think of this as conversational chess.

Unsurprisingly, Jean turned to Blair. Because, at this moment, she surely liked Blair more.

"I hear a hint of the Midwest in your voice," Jean said. "Wisconsin?"

"I'm from Iowa," Blair said. "You?"

"Wyoming. But I'm obsessed with the heartland. And finally, last year, I went to Wisconsin."

"What did you shoot?"

"At the top of the state, there's a town of seven hundred. Bayfield. A little arts community—the Provincetown of Wisconsin. Every fall, they have an apple festival, and ten or twenty thousand people show up. And at the end, a dozen high school bands march down Main Street playing 'On, Wisconsin!' People weep."

I couldn't not speak. "Jean Coin took pictures of weeping cheeseheads?"

"It's about the shot from the bottom of the hill as the bands come down . . . it's an abstraction, an avalanche of color."

Blair shifted the topic. "Wyoming's so beautiful. Why did you leave?"

"Same reason you left Iowa."

"Somehow I don't think you came to New York to study international business at Columbia."

"Pre-law at Princeton. Same idea."

"I wouldn't have guessed that. How did you get from law to photography?"

"I never tell this story."

Blair turned to me. "I think Jean has a great story to tell us. Don't you, David?"

"You have a request from the floor," I said. "Which I second."

"You asked for it." Jean drained her coffee. "My father was the irrigator for a ranch. I grew up riding the owner's horses. People think it's all Western saddle and rodeos and riding the range out there, but it isn't—they ride English too. It turned out I was an absolute whiz. At sixteen, I was probably the best jumper in Wyoming and Montana. And I got good grades. There was some press. Princeton gave me a full scholarship. So I went."

"And?"

"I'd never been east. Princeton—the whole scene—blew my mind. Especially my first competition. It was huge, like every rider in New Jersey was there. I'm sure I was the only one who didn't have her own horse. I looked at the girls who rode ahead of me, and I saw: They were better. They'd had every advantage, and then they'd worked hard. I couldn't handle it—I'd always been the gold standard. I clutched. I went on automatic."

"How'd you do?"

"This is where it gets crazy. If I were scoring it, I'd say fourth. Maybe third. But I won. I couldn't believe it. The other girls couldn't either. You should see the picture of me accepting the trophy—talk about stunned. Anyway, I go to take my horse in, and there's this kid waiting for me: Ben Griesman. We have a class together. Maybe I've nodded hello to him. But we've never spoken. 'Nice going,' he says. I say, 'I didn't deserve to win.' 'You're right,' he says, 'but the judge with the rummy nose thought you did.' I ask how he knew that. 'Because I fixed the judging,' he says. And then he tells me how he went to the judge and promised the guy he'd have a date with me that night if I won. I couldn't begin to know how to have a conversation like that. But this eighteen-year-old Princeton freshman whose idea of a horse was a nag in front of a carriage on Central Park South—he knew how to bribe a judge."

"Why did he do it?" Blair asked.

"I asked him. And he says, 'I saw you in class and I thought . . . I felt . . . I know you. You're like me.' I had to laugh. I say, 'Are you nuts? My father doesn't own a suit to be buried in.' He says, 'You're a storybook girl. You want it all, and you're meant to have it.' I say, 'Including dinner with an old drunk? What else did you promise him?' And he goes, 'He knows I'm meeting you after dinner.'"

Blair, fascinated, gestured for more.

"And he looked at me, like he really did know me, and I felt something break inside, this wave of incredible relief, and I just . . . went to him. He bought me my first camera. We were together for five years."

Blair couldn't get enough. "And then?"

"I was home for the summer. The owners of the ranch had a friend visiting. She wanted to ride, so I took her up into the national forest. We climbed and climbed, and when she saw that the eagles were flying below us, she wanted to stop. Then she kissed me. And . . ."

Silence. Interrupted by chess pieces clicking on concrete tables. And birds. And the distant sounds of football and baseball on the Great Lawn. And, finally, by Blair.

"So this thing we might do together . . . you've done it before?"

"This . . . *thing*?" I read Jean's smile as quizzical. "Yes. I have."

"And . . ."

"Each time . . . when it was over . . . the same word described the quality of the pleasure . . . *annihilating*." Jean drew it out, making it sound like the ultimate contentment.

I imagined the three of us, sheets rumpled, overwhelmed by what we'd done. And the sense of freedom, feeling no sin, anticipating no punishment. I looked over at Blair, and I could see she was reassured by Jean's answer. And pleased that Jean would be her guide.

I was stunned by what Blair did next. She stood, leaned over the table, put a hand to Jean's cheek, and kissed her, softly, but in not any way timidly, on the mouth.

"So, we seem to agree," I said, when the kiss ended. "Saturday?"

"Works for me," Jean said. "Downtown okay?"

"Downtown's best."

"Why?"

I wanted all the physical intimacy but nothing more. A quick exit limited the possibility of an emotional connection.

"If we come to you," I said, "I'm sure we'll all wake up in our own beds."

A knowing smile from Jean. Kiss, kiss on the cheeks for me. Kiss, kiss for Blair—also on the cheeks. And, like that, Jean was gone.

She left a vacuum. I felt an awkwardness. Blair seemed to feel it too, for we took our coffee cups to the trash in silence.

"Someone is full of surprises," I said.

"Someone surprised herself."

"A good surprise?" I asked, a sliver of jealously in my question.

"Yes," she said. "But not annihilating."

CHAPTER 12

"Da-vid."

Victoria. On the phone, Monday morning at nine, she's ready to play whatever role is needed: law partner, office wife, moral compass.

"I'm starting to miss you, V."

"Indian summer—it goes on and on."

"I don't hear oars cutting smoothly through water."

"I'm sitting in a lawn chair, looking at the boat."

"Sloth . . . or injury?"

"Too much of last night, I'm afraid."

"Color me shocked."

"Me too." She paused. "I've got a . . . suitor." Her voice turned girlish. "You'd like him, David."

"Should I have him checked out?"

"No need. I've known him forever."

"Spill."

"Johnny Metcalfe."

"No bells ring," I said.

"Before your time, I handled his divorce. He remarried. A long, happy marriage followed, ended by a brief, ugly illness. You know the short story about a wife dying and women who never knew her showing up at the funeral to comfort the husband? After Ginny died, it was like that. Johnny stopped dating when one woman after another told him she'd only sleep with him if he asked her to marry him. He went alone to a dinner on Saturday night, and there I was—interested neither in sleeping with him, at least initially, or marriage, ever."

"That's lovely, V. I'm happy for you."

"Early days, David. How was your weekend?"

"It was . . ." I have never lied to this woman; I couldn't start now. "Domestic."

Which was, technically, true.

CHAPTER 13

Taped to my phone is a line from Norman Mailer:

You don't really know a woman until you meet her in court.

I trust Mailer on this—he was married six times.

Do I "know" Blair? Not really. Not fully. Not, anyway, in the kind of soul merger I thought was possible when we were first married, living in a third-floor walk-up, and I'd rush home each night to ravish my bride.

In my experience, those who believe in the possibility of a soul marriage gush, overshare, and expect you to do the same. Another way to put it: They're unhinged. Like the woman in "Suzanne." Whenever I hear that song, I think of all that's left unsaid. Yes, she takes you down to her place by the river, she feeds you tea and oranges, and it seems like you've always been her lover. Dreamy. Poetic. Possibly exalted. Overlooked: that "she's half crazy." Which, really, is obvious. Talk, sex, talk, more sex, and then it's dawn—who can live like that, night after night?

Not me.

And not Blair.

Over the past two decades, I've come to know a great deal about her, but I can't say I've learned much more than I knew when we got married. Family, school, favorite books and movies, the first boyfriend, and later, the first love—I know all the facts that don't really matter.

What would I like to know about her?

Everything she's mentioned in passing and then turned away from, as if she wished she hadn't said anything—that "memorable" party when she was sixteen, the summer in Paris with her best friend after her freshman year, and what happened in a parked car in a downpour on Cape Cod just before she came to New York for business school.

From time to time, at random moments when she's least expecting it, I've asked Blair some impertinent questions.

"Ever get drunk and wake up in a room you've never seen before?"

"Ever ask God for help . . . and get it?"

"Ever do it in a bedroom on coats?"

"Ever steal anything bigger than a hair clip from a drugstore?"

"Could you shoot to kill?"

"Ever go to a gay bar—a bar for gay women?"

Every one of these questions produced silence.

A few years ago, on our anniversary, I said, "I don't think I'll ever get to know you better than I do now."

"Are you okay with that?"

"Yes."

"Smart."

My answer was weak. And it was a lie. Of course I'd like to know more. You spend your life with someone, how can you not be curious?

I found a way to get information from Blair: in bed. I only get snippets. They're not volunteered. I wait until we're intensely involved and communicating in shorthand— "yes," "more," and "don't stop" mostly—and then I throw out a question.

"What was the shortest time between meeting a guy and going home with him?"

"A club." Blair's eyes are closed. "The coat check. On the way in."

"You didn't go in?"

"No."

"When was this?"

"Three months before I met you."

My idea of hot is Blair's idea of cold, so I asked no follow-up questions. Was I satisfied? Not really. The more you know, the more you want to know. Like how that night played out. In detail. What was she wearing? What happened in the cab? Was there kissing? Touching? Whose apartment did they go to? When they got there, did they get to the bed or just drop to the floor? How many times? Did they spend the night, make a plan, see each other again? Was he big?

Later—weeks and weeks later—we were having what we call a "single malt night." Blair likes wine; I drink it only at meals. But once in a great while, because our total intent is to get drunk and then go at it in ways we pretend not to remember in the morning, we drink shot after shot of single malt.

Semi-blotto from the whiskey, I was concentrating on a two-inch area of Blair when I flashed on the night she never made it into the club. And I thought: Maybe I can get one question in. Instinct said: Don't return to that night; she'll feel set up, sorry she said anything.

So I asked a general question: "Does size count?"

"Yes. Oh, yes."

"What's more important: length or width?"

"Width."

I stopped there. Wisely.

That was one of our best nights ever.

The week before we were to get together with Jean, I had trouble concentrating. I didn't want Blair to know I was counting the hours, so I maintained my usual weekday schedule: work, gym, a business dinner, a bit of reading, snatches of conversation, *The Daily Show*. Surprisingly, no sex. Kissing, hugs, sleep. It felt like I was on a training regimen—storing energy, building strength.

That could only last so long. On Thursday night, bored by an interview with a dinosaur of a politician, we switched to a black-and-white movie, smoked, and tumbled into bed.

I began a monologue that I had, with variations, delivered on nights like this for at least a decade.

"Blair," I whispered.

Her response was slow, distant. "Yes."

"We're in the dressing room at Bergdorf's . . ."

"Yes?"

"This dress . . . I like it. . . . Do you?"

"Yes."

"Oh, and here's the salesgirl."

Blair, breathy as Marilyn Monroe, volleyed: "Salesgirl?"

"With another dress . . . she wants to help you."

All the while, I was stroking Blair's thighs.

"What does she look like?"

"Short hair . . . big breasts . . . I think she's Russian."

Setting it down here, that scene is ludicrous. But when it's dark and late and you're toasted, it's easy and pleasant to role-play. And Blair seemed to be doing just that, arching her back as I moved my hands to her breasts, thumbs brushing her nipples.

"She wants . . ."

An abrupt end to the fantasy—Blair opened her eyes and laughed. Raucous laughter. Derisive laughter.

"Sorry, that's just so . . . ridiculous."

"You used to like that fantasy," I said.

"Only the first hundred times."

"You never said no."

My hand stopped making lazy patterns on Blair's thigh. She sat up and caressed my face.

"I hurt your feelings," she said.

"You took me by surprise."

"Oh, honey." She kissed me. "You just can't wait for Saturday, can you?"

I felt transparent as a four-year-old.

"No. How about you?"

"Some anticipation. But not like you. You've been thinking . . . disgusting thoughts, haven't you?"

I nodded.

"And you thought you could hide them?" Blair pulled me close. "My poor darling beast, come and do horrible things to me."

CHAPTER 14

"You want to get divorced—why?"

It's the first thing I ask new clients. Not out of curiosity, or to help me build their cases, but because . . . maybe they shouldn't.

Most matrimonial lawyers, like most other professionals, choose their trade for the fees. Clients enter, on a conveyor belt, married; they leave, sheared of a few illusions, divorced. The trick is to make that happen in the greatest number of billable hours but with the fewest possible strokes.

Some matrimonial lawyers still have ideals. They'll get you unhitched, but first they'll test you to see if there's still life in your marriage. Like first-stage marriage counselors.

I'm in that group. I listen to my clients' stories, and when I hear descriptions of marriages that are retrievable, I encourage these women to try couples therapy. They wonder why. The husband doesn't listen, he has disgusting habits, he pays no attention to the kids, how can anyone stay married to a man like this?

Yes, I say, he's a slob, a jerk. But please notice there's something you don't complain about, and that's sex.

If you're still having sex, you can save the marriage.

If the sex has gone, it's over.

A woman laments that her husband has become her "best friend," and the euphemism tells me all I need to know. "Friend" is what's left when the sex goes. So that's a dead marriage.

A woman says she's learned to schedule her husband's desire for sex: "one night on, two nights off." She doesn't need to say more. For her, sex is an obligation that can't be ignored but can be managed. And that's a dead marriage.

A woman complains that her husband has a lover, but she doesn't complain about the lover to him, or get interested in his interests, or buy hot lingerie. For her, it's a relief that he strays. Another dead marriage.

And then there's roommate marriage. Victoria calls this condition "low batt," meaning low sexual battery, no erotic sparks. The husband's nights are about the flat screen; weekends mean the golf course. His wife? A client told me, speaking for many, "No man has ever given me as much pleasure as I get slapping my Amex card down on a counter at Bloomingdale's."

Some women complain about their oversexed husbands. I never comment. Whatever their issue is, it's an issue for a therapist. But I have to suppress a renegade impulse to share how many men have told me that the last time their wives went down on them was the night before their wedding— and to follow that up with a question: How long has it been since you had your husband in your mouth?

And another query, just as rude: Given that life is short and youth is fleeting, why have you stayed in a sexless marriage for so long that you've forgotten you're entitled to pleasure? Because you have kids and your husband is a good father? That's a lesson you want to pass on to those children? Really?

I want to shout at my clients: "Sex *isn't* how you say thanks to the guy who pays your rent. It *isn't* what you give up when you become a parent. It *isn't* what you ration, and it *isn't* what you live without because you don't want your kids to grow up in a broken home."

Sex is, at the very least, the reward we get for surviving

the day; at the very most, it's the life force. It's intimate touch, souls connecting through flesh. It's magic. Without a sex drive that seeks and finds fulfillment, you might as well be like a brain creature in an old sci-fi movie—a head unencumbered by a body.

What's most infuriating is how persistent the belief is that great sex is rare, or difficult, or available only to those with secret knowledge. Bullshit. Great lovers may or may not have Olympian bodies and great technique. What they must have—all they must have—is interest. Just that. The willingness to pleasure another. A commitment to the beloved's joy.

So I make no apologies for anything I do—for anything Blair and I do—to keep sex hot year after year. I can't put it on a résumé, but on my list of achievements, somewhere below father to Ann and far above winning fair settlements for my clients, would be two decades of marriage with our sex lives in no danger of cooling.

That's why getting together with Jean Coin didn't make me worry that Blair and I were risking our marriage, or really, risking anything. Jean was an adventure. A new twist on an old recipe. Harmless fun. And nobody's business but ours.

CHAPTER 15

You would think we weren't speaking, the way Blair and I avoided each other on Saturday.

I woke early, made coffee, brought some to my barely awake wife, and fled to the gym. From there, I went to the office, where I confronted a stack of work that could have easily waited until Monday. I ordered soup and read the *Financial Times'* Weekend section. I did not watch a single porn video, and at the moment I thought I might, I left the office and walked across the park.

Home. There were clothes in neat piles on the bed—candidates for what Blair would wear to Jean's—but no Blair.

I showered. Shaved. Twice. Considered going out and buying some Axe, the better to be irresistible. Thought better of it. Went into Ann's room to watch college football. The cheerleaders were more compelling than the game. Napped.

When I woke, there was music—jaunty Mozart flute concertos—and Blair was sitting on the couch, her hair wet from the shower, reading and sipping wine.

For a few seconds, I stood in the hall, watching and thinking: Forget the striped cotton sweater, the short denim skirt, and the weightless suede jacket—the most beautiful woman really is a woman reading a book.

Which was quickly followed by: Is it possible that the last time I thought this was just three weeks ago?

Then I stepped into my marriage.

"Hey."

Blair looked up from the book. Smiled. I leaned over, and we kissed, a real kiss, with a lot of feeling behind it.

The book surprised me. "A cookbook?"

"Better than fiction—every recipe has a happy ending."

"Want me to cook something before we go?" I asked.

"Vanity dictates a flat stomach."

"I understand. But I see tequila in your future. Or champagne. You'll want a base. Yogurt, at the very least."

"How about . . . stir-fry?"

"Good. I'll make it."

"Thanks," Blair said. "One favor."

"Yes?"

"No garlic."

In the cab, we rode in silence, far apart, staring blankly ahead, thoughtful.

"We must look like the couple in that *American Gothic* painting," I said, as we started the long drive downtown. "All we need is the pitchfork."

"Please. We are hip New Yorkers."

"Not that hip," I said. "We could still bail. Go home, pull a movie."

Blair shook her head.

"Why not?" I asked.

"You've got a script, don't you?"

"Excuse me?"

"Positions. Sequences. Who does what."

"So?"

"So let's do this."

"Do *you* have a script?" I asked.

"No. But I don't want to spend the rest of my life hearing about the fun we missed."

"You really see fun ahead?"

"What I know of your fantasies—and by now I think I've heard them all—they're vanilla. So I don't see *harm*. And I think Jean is . . ."

Blair searched for the right word. "Harmless?" I suggested.

"Cool," she said.

Well, that was a surprise. But not one that registered. I was thinking ahead, to the dance of bodies. And to an agreement I'd failed to make explicit. I waited until the cab reached Tribeca to mention it.

"When I need to come, I want to be in you."

"Okay."

"Don't . . . wander off."

We got out on Greenwich, a few blocks from Jean's loft. On this warm Saturday night, the young were everywhere—filling the sidewalk café in front of Locanda Verde, smoking outside De Niro's hotel. They were groomed. Expensively underdressed. They wore scents that broadcast self-confidence. And discretionary money. Hard to look at these kids and not feel jealous. Also: old.

We turned onto Laight Street, a movie set of old warehouses converted to condos and new condos designed to look like they were once warehouses. I'd imagined Jean living in a loft like the ones I knew when I was in law school and one of my girlfriends lived down here—wood floors that were a minefield of splinters, exposed water pipes, clawfoot bathtub and noisy plumbing. But there was no modestly improved industrial space left in Tribeca.

I was forced to readjust; Jean had money.

And not just some—more than we have.

From an open window, party sounds emerged. And music: "Almost Saturday Night," written, sung, and produced by John Fogerty, who labored over his breakthrough songs, he said, because he didn't want to go back to working at the car wash. And here he was, party music for the privileged.

It had been years since we danced. I grabbed Blair and held her close. Then she broke away, and for a few seconds, she found the beat and went with it. I'd almost forgotten how hot Blair was when she moved.

I pressed Jean's bell.

CHAPTER 16

A massive photo in the lobby. Not Jean's. She'd never shoot such sentimental chlorophyll: Central Park, three miles and several cultures north, in full summer.

The elevator. Holding hands with Blair. Nervous smiles.

Jean's building, for all its pin lighting and polished brick, was venerable in one respect. One loft per floor, so when the elevator opens, you step right into the living space.

We did.

And found ourselves alone.

The living area was vast, big enough for an energetic game of floor hockey. And almost empty. By the elevator, a simple white table with a concise collection of refreshment opportunities. Hardly any furniture: a couch, two Eames chairs, a low table, and a dark Persian rug. Near the kitchen area, a pine table and a few cane chairs. A bookcase on a distant wall. Large, framed photographs everywhere, none of them by Jean. Gauze curtains over the massive windows. No overhead lights, and the few lamps had dimmers set low.

From faraway speakers, a Southern woman was listing her troubles, her voice rough and ageless and bearing the terrible history of Alabama or Mississippi. The song was blues—*Why do I worry, why do I have to cry? Why do I have to carry this heavy load?*—delivered slowly, accompanied by a slide guitar. It registered as a sexy, smoldering strut.

I called out: "Jean?"

No response.

"Feels like the start of *Law and Order*," I whispered. "Let's find the body."

Jean emerged from the back of the apartment, so far away we had plenty of time to adjust, to gawk, to think of some clever greeting. And, most of all, to appreciate Jean's sense of drama. In her own home, she was making an entrance.

"*Y Tu Mamá También*," Blair murmured.

Do you know this movie? Made in Mexico, it's the story of two teenage boys and a lovely woman in her thirties who go on a road trip together, and on their last night at a secluded beach, they go to a dive bar and get sloppy drunk. The woman puts coins in the jukebox. Music starts, slow, loose-hipped, rapturous. She shimmies her way back to the table and takes the boys in hand. They start to dance. Only it's not really dancing. With the woman in the middle, they grind in a way that makes it absolutely clear they'll only need one bed tonight.

Jean wasn't quite dancing, but she was definitely feeling the music. She was in uniform—white shirt and jeans—but with her shirt half-unbuttoned, which surely had something to do with whatever she was sipping.

"David."

A brief kiss on the mouth. She stepped back, set the glass on the table.

"Blair."

Another brief kiss on the mouth.

Jean stepped back, her focus still on Blair.

"May I?"

The question was a formality. Blair wasn't really being asked anything.

Jean placed her right hand on Blair's hip. She made no move to pull Blair closer—it looked as if they were doing some formal eighteenth-century dance.

Then Jean slipped her hand under Blair's skirt.

Surprise for me.

Surprise for Jean.

Blair was naked underneath.

"Oh," Jean murmured. "Delicious."

I thought Jean would start to stroke Blair, but she didn't—she was cupping Blair between her legs, concentrating the warmth of her hand.

Blair looked stricken, stunned. This was so fast, so unexpected, so direct.

"Just for a minute," Jean whispered.

Jean's hand was doing nothing; it was just a statement of fact. Of a deep understanding. Of a kind of possession. Energy from one woman flowing to the other. And back.

Eyes closed, Blair looked drugged, far away. She couldn't resist this. She opened her legs. Tensed. Shuddered. Gasped. Shuddered again. Sighed.

Jean withdrew her hand.

Blair opened her eyes. She looked disoriented, as if she'd suddenly been awakened from a nap.

"That was . . . something."

Jean gently put her hand against Blair's cheek. "That was breaking the ice," Jean said.

"Melting the ice," I said.

Jean smiled. "Can you stand it, David?"

"I could have watched that for hours."

"Really?" Blair laughed. "Just standing there?"

"Drink?" Jean said.

She poured tequila.

Jean carried the bottle and kept our glasses filled as she gave us the photo tour, with terse commentary that explained why she chose the Cartier-Bresson of Muslim women praying in Pakistan in 1949, the reason for the Meyerowitz of Cape Cod Bay at dusk, and the importance of the huge Gursky landscape. There was a theme: the horizon. Not just as the dividing line between earth and sky but what the idea of the horizon means to pilots and photographers: Don't get distracted; look straight ahead. And what it means in relationships: Be completely present, look a person in the eye.

By then, we'd reached the far end of the living room. We'd had two or three shots of tequila and had smoked an astonishingly potent joint. The music had changed to something African, sung by women in French, with guitars that snaked around a slow, hypnotic beat.

Blair looked relaxed, like whatever came next would prove to be more like a pleasant party than a watershed event.

Jean led us around a corner and into her bedroom. It could not have been simpler. King-size bed, with a thick white duvet that suggested a four-figure thread count. Candles, carafes, and water glasses on side tables. Speakers bolted to the walls.

Blair smiled at Jean, who giggled. They had the same thought, and I was it. Blair unbuttoned my shirt. Jean loosened my belt. I kicked off my moccasins. In seconds, I was naked.

Blair watched as Jean reached for me.

Her hand was like a mouth.

"Unfair," I murmured, but not as a complaint.

Jean kneeled and took me between her lips. Blair kneeled. Jean knew why and, with a slow final lick, released me. Blair took over. Then they switched. And again. Then with one variation: Like a woman with two mouths, they licked me together.

And that was just sport. Soon enough, they got serious, taking turns with me in their mouths. I closed my eyes. I couldn't tell who was doing what.

The pleasure was intense beyond anything I had ever experienced. I felt I could come, and I knew I didn't want to.

"Please . . . no," I whispered, and they stopped. "Get up."

They stood. Jean and I stripped Blair. Blair and I stripped Jean. I don't know why it seemed important that we stay standing up, that we not tumble onto the bed, but it was a good idea—Jean and I sucked Blair's nipples. Blair and I sucked Jean's. We shared a three-way kiss. I stood behind Blair and rested my hand between her legs, as Jean pressed her nipples against Blair's. And then Blair and I did that to Jean.

"Want to give David a show?"

Blair stiffened. "Can it be . . . darker?"

Jean blew out one of the candles and led Blair to the bed. "Lie down. On your back, like you were going to sleep. Head on the pillow . . . and open your legs."

Blair did. Jean did the same but lying in the opposite direction, her head at the foot of the bed. They looked like matching snow angels—until Jean positioned herself so she and Blair were scissored together, legs locked, sex pressed tight against sex.

This was Jean's show, and soon I could see why. She had brought Blair to a quick orgasm; now it was her turn. And, in bed with a woman, this was clearly how she liked to get off.

Jean looked joyous, fantasy realized, release on the way.

Blair's eyes were shut tight. She wasn't enjoying this. She'd signed up for the beginners' course, only to be bumped up to an advanced class. It was in her nature to want to do well, and she wasn't, by her standard, succeeding.

Blair whispered, "Jean?"

Jean was too deep into it to answer.

I heard Blair's distress but didn't feel I should intervene. Yet. "Jean, I need to . . ."

Now Jean heard. And understood. On the cusp of orgasm, she stopped short. She sat, took Blair by the wrists, and pulled her up.

"I am so sorry," Jean said.

"It's just . . ."

"Too much for a first time. And David must be feeling left out." Jean turned to me. "Though he doesn't seem to be pouting."

"Are you okay?" Blair asked me.

"I could have watched that for hours."

"Enough with the watching," Jean said. "Shall we make David very, very happy?"

In a sentence, Jean had recast the triangle as a twosome: adultery with a witness and occasional co-conspirator. Now I was in charge. No pressure on Blair. Deft.

A man and his wish list. Early Christmas.

Before they started working me over, I sensed that Jean liked to have an orgasm before she fucked, so I put my face between her legs and gave her one.

Blair's eyes glittered.

"Want some?" I asked.

She nodded.

I turned to Jean. I didn't have to say anything. The two of us, giving Blair the night of her life—no question, we had the same fantasy.

Jean and I stood over Blair. Eyes slowly scanning, taking one another in. Anticipation was physical: pounding heart, slow breathing. A buzz in the air, desire crackling, and powerful forces at work.

I felt a kind of awe at what we might create together. Then Jean and I plunged.

There were places we didn't go. I didn't ask Blair to go down on Jean. I didn't suggest that Jean—or Blair—use the strap-on that had to be in the drawer of the table by the side of the bed. Or that Blair do much of anything while I was with Jean.

We'd arrived at some unspoken ground rules, making sure everyone was included and no one got hurt.

Blair, Jean—at any moment, did it make a difference who I was loving? There was enough to go around. More than enough; we were in a zone of abundance. Four breasts. Six hands. Many of each and yet not too much. A thought: If you can have this, who would choose less?

We paused for more tequila for Jean and me, water for Blair. We held one another and kissed. There was so much more to do, and yet . . . and yet I felt almost ready to come and go. But why? Why did I feel so . . . drained?

Because every touch was searing. Because as I lost myself in these women, I felt I was losing myself in myself—swirling, spinning, corkscrewing my way into unknown emotional territory. In all my scenarios, developed over years, I'd failed to realize that sex with two people was fundamentally the same as sex with one person but twice as intense. As a physical event, it was a riot of sensation, an electrical connection with multiple plugs and sockets. And very much an emotional connection. Even more emotional than physical.

"Jean, would you mind if I . . . finish with Blair?"

She didn't. Jean Coin, the consummate hostess.

"My darling," Blair said as I entered her.

I whispered in her ear, "Dear God, how I love you."

We moved together, the way we do. Blair didn't come, but it didn't matter—in a room not our own, we were together. Unshakably together.

When we were finished, I lay in Jean's bed and thought that what we'd done had opened me up to a new way of feeling. Everything seemed different. Clearer. Life seemed more . . . spacious. I'm not saying this exactly right, but what started with sex—what I thought was only about sex— seemed to have ended up very far from it.

CHAPTER 17

We lay in bed, silent, recovering, just breathing.

The music was on a loop. The blues song we'd heard when we arrived began again.

"Seems like a year ago," Blair said. "Who is that?"

"Big Mama Thornton."

I sensed that Jean knew a great deal about Big Mama and could have launched into the particulars of her career, but I didn't want to be educated, just to nap. Blair sat up. I reached for a glass of water.

And just like that the party was over.

Blair and I started to assemble our clothes.

Jean, wrapped in the sheets, seemed surprised. "David . . . you're *leaving*?"

"I'm not one of those guys who can do this all night."

"You're kidding," Jean said.

Blair giggled as she slipped on her sweater. "If David and I have a really intense encounter, he not only doesn't want to do it again, he says he'll *never* want to do it again."

"No!"

"It's true," I said. "I tell Blair, 'Well, that's *that*. Take the rest of your life off.'"

"But you know better," Jean said.

"At that moment, it's the truth. I gave Blair everything I had. And I can't imagine ever wanting more."

"How many nights before he's hot for you again?" Jean asked.

"One," Blair said, and both women laughed. "But after tonight . . . two . . . maybe three."

"What about you, Blair?" Jean asked. "You're really done?"

"I was once with a guy who said, 'I can go all night.' I told him, 'Please, don't.' So I'm with David a hundred and ten percent on this one." She paused. "On pretty much everything, actually."

"Got it," Jean said, and kissed me.

But she couldn't resist provoking. As Blair and I finished dressing, Jean untangled herself from the top sheet and stood. Naked.

Now that we were on the far side of sex, even a bare breast was unsettling to Blair. Jean read the moment and found a T-shirt.

Count on Blair, the college dean, to know how to end an evening on good terms. She hugged Jean. "This was special. Thank you."

"My pleasure," Jean said.

"And mine," I said. "In a very big way, mine."

"I'm glad," Jean said.

"Really," I said. "That was so good, it's a miracle it's legal."

We kissed—on the cheeks—at the door.

"Safe travels," Jean said, as if we weren't taking the elevator and a cab uptown but were going on an ocean voyage.

"You too," Blair said.

"Send postcards," I added, a line so silly that we all laughed, and then the elevator opened.

"You okay?"

"Yes," Blair said.

"Fun?"

"Interesting."

"Uh-oh."

"Yes, fun." Blair punched me lightly. "Can you hold off on the recap for a *minute*?"

The elevator released us. We stepped into the night, the air cooler, the party music now softer. As one, we took a breath.

"It's early. Want a drink?"

"So much," Blair said. "But let's walk a bit."

"We did that just right," I said.

"What is 'right'?"

"You spend the night, you're in a relationship. You leave, you've made no commitment."

"That's a little . . . pat, don't you think?"

Another sentence I never thought would come out of my mouth in this lifetime: "I read that in an etiquette piece about threesomes on the web."

Blair was amused. "You *studied* threesomes?"

"I started to read some pieces."

"What stopped you?"

"The first piece I read answered every question."

"Like?"

"What to do and say after the final orgasm."

"Let me guess." Blair looked into the distance, as if she might find the answer etched on the sky. "*Thanks, great time, let's get together again sometime.*"

"Wow. Exactly. How did—"

"Maybe I read the same piece," Blair said, and hers was the very model of a wicked smile.

"What other homework did you do?"

"I watched some videos on tribbing," she said.

"Tribbing?"

"That scissoring thing we did when Jean and I were on the bed, facing away from each other."

"That thing you stopped doing."

"Your favorite moment, no doubt."

"Well, it was new."

"And?"

"Scorching hot. Two beautiful women . . ."

"One in better shape than the other," Blair said. I was still returning to Earth. Blair was back in New York, measuring, comparing, judging. "Jean made me feel like I should go to the gym more."

"Don't do it for me. In fact . . ."

I slid my hand under Blair's skirt and cupped her ass. It turned out she wasn't quite finished for the night. I wasn't either. We walked to the Village, had two drinks each, and took a cab home, where, to my surprise, I was eager for another round with Blair.

CHAPTER 18

Hidden in the Metro section of the Sunday *Times* is a feature called "Sunday Routine" that chronicles, hour by hour, how prominent New Yorkers spend their day off.

Almost without exception, these people used to sleep in on Sundays. Then they got dogs—from shelters, they're quick to say—and now their pets rouse them early, so their day begins with walks in the park. They have coffee in mugs—always in mugs—and read the paper. The real paper, the paper paper. Food is optional. Maybe toast or oatmeal. They catch up on Facebook posts and are surprised by how many "friends" they've acquired since they last checked. They hit the gym and the flea market; Zabar's is a frequent destination. Night falls and, at last, they feed. Fish. Kale. Wakame, nine-grain Japanese rice, salmon roe for protein. Their wild excess? A shared dessert. A favorite show on TV, saved for Sunday night. A book. Then sleep, surrounded by dogs.

These are rich, textured lives, and these people are, for all their prominence, surprisingly restrained. No lunch at Balthazar or Swifty's. No jaunts in the Jaguar to hang with hedge funders in Greenwich. And most of all: no sex. Partners, lovers, and spouses are mentioned, but carnal activity is omitted. Relationships are presented as old shoes. And someone always goes to sleep earlier.

Our Sundays are different.

We had the dream child: no desire for pets, plants, or any Disney destination. So even when Ann was here, Blair slept in on Sundays. I'd be up early, clear a week's worth of personal email, and—I was an English major, so old habits die hard—read the paper, the real paper, marking the articles I thought Blair shouldn't miss. At nine, using an old-fashioned espresso machine, I'd make Blair a double shot and deliver it to her with the paper. I'd pay bills and read about investing, which I'm not good at but want to be. Ann, afflicted with teenage narcolepsy, would wake up at eleven, text her friends, hit me up for money, and abandon us for the day.

Since Ann left, we've been spending Sundays on the street. After soup and a sandwich, we head out, walking fast, destination unknown, returning at dusk. Dinner is pasta with vegetables. A long bath for Blair. Beer and the last football game of the weekend for me. Then a short, friendly session in bed—what a friend calls "fucking lite"—and dreamland.

Decades of fantasy and anticipation, then you get what you wanted—not surprising that I felt drained and slept late. Blair, up early, seemed frazzled. I read this as a delayed reaction. What kind of reaction . . . I didn't know. And I wanted to. So I brought espresso and settled into bed next to her.

The way to begin this conversation required delicacy, tact, and finesse. Instead, I said, "My head is full of sentences that are so amazing to me I can't quite accept them as true."

"Like?"

Where I was coming from: adolescence, the sequel. In my head, this was exactly the right time to review the night's highlight reel. Like this was a panel on ESPN.

"I watched a woman go down on my wife. I fucked another woman while my wife watched. I fucked my wife while another woman sucked her nipples."

"I was there. Stop."

"Okay. But you'll note that *my wife* was in every sentence."

Blair was starting to smolder. "Well, you were very careful that way."

"Careful?"

"You made sure I was always included."

"Nothing 'careful' about it—that was the whole point."

What was this? Blair felt set up? It couldn't be; Blair wasn't someone who rewrote the past and then insisted it had always been just that way.

I thought: It must be something else. And it was.

"If it had been what Jean wanted, just the two of you," Blair said, "would that have been better?"

"No."

"Just as good?"

"No."

"Why not?"

"Because . . . because last night was about more than getting off."

"There was *more*?" And how I would like to report that Blair's tone might be called quizzical. "Last night was *entirely* about getting off."

"There was no *idea* involved?"

"Oh. Right. An idea: 'It's not cheating if your wife's there,'" Blair said, quoting me, her tone tight. "Not exactly a ringing endorsement of monogamy."

But it was, my darling. And it is. And that is not news to you. That view—that *idea*, if you will—is the distilla-

tion of more than a decade of labor in the fields of matrimonial law. You have heard me work these ideas out over
many dinners. And you have watched me struggle—for my
clients, for myself, and perhaps, though I have no way of
knowing because you keep so much of yourself private, for
you—with the challenge of monogamy.

Because if we're honest, every time we look at an attractive person, we think: I wonder what it would be like to . . .

And so I figured, at least in theory, I had found a way
for couples—for some couples—to relieve the pressure of
monogamy without wrecking a marriage.

"Look at us," I said. "Is our marriage weaker or stronger
today? I say stronger. I fucked another woman while my
wife watched—and the world didn't end. My wife—"

"*Stop it!*"

"And another woman—"

"Shut the fuck up! I mean it! *Not another word!*"

My parents are screamers. As a kid, I found their rage
terrifying—ten-minute thunderstorms that came without
warning and ended just as abruptly, never to be mentioned
again. Those blitzes made me fear all domestic upsets. That's
one reason I bonded with Blair. She's the opposite of my
mother: steady, considerate, and slow to anger. Outbursts
are not her thing. Snark is. And when she's in that mode,

picking you apart with nasty little comments, you might almost wish for rage.

"Okay," I said. "Okay." I got out of bed, grabbed last night's clothes, and disappeared to the farthest corner of the apartment to try and figure out what had happened to Blair while we slept.

Jared called. Blair said we weren't going out, so he came over. Jared likes football, so he watched the Giants game with me. Blair, in a better mood, joined us.

Jared doesn't work. He doesn't have to. In his twenties, he invented a kids' dessert called Frozen Fruit Guts—the flavors were Rotten Raspberry, Mushy Melon, and Grisly Grape—that he sold to one of the biggest food companies for a fortune. He went on to write short, funny books (*Feminism in Sicily* and *Last Chiropractor Before Freeway*) before hitting some kind of personal wall. His last writing, if you can call it that, involved naming racehorses for friends (Long Shot Kick the Bucket and Rocking Horse Winner). He's stuck, maybe unraveling. But with a live audience, he can be as witty and ironic as he was when we met him.

That Jared is Blair's best friend makes total sense—Jared is gay. Many women with busy or inattentive husbands have a friend like this; the man is never going to hit on her, and she is never going to suggest that what they have is really so much deeper than friendship. And her husband approves.

I *more* than approve. I *like* Jared. In a city where you hear two opinions on any topic but rarely a third, Jared throws off one fresh opinion after another. I'd never watched football with him, and I couldn't imagine he liked to spend a Sunday afternoon watching sports, but here he was. And here was his offering as a broadcast analyst: "Football is a gay pageant."

Who would we rather listen to—the Fox announcer or Jared? No contest. We muted the sound.

Jared's voice is a rich baritone, but he pushed it deeper. "The offensive line assumes the position. The quarterback presses himself against the center . . ."

His repertoire wasn't infinite, or maybe there's only so much innuendo that football can support. After a few plays, he called it quits.

Blair took over.

"Oh, look," she said, in an exact imitation of Jared. "The tight end is going deep. The quarterback hits him, and . . . he's in!"

We laughed, applauded Blair, traded football for a movie with subtitles, and ordered Chinese takeout: egg roll (170 calories), Kung Pao Chicken (434 calories per cup, 63 percent of them fat), and Tsingtao beer (153 calories). Somewhere in there was protein. Jared, thin as a stick, had three bowls of chicken.

In the evening, Ann made her Sunday call. Liked her classes, liked her dorm, still liked her high school boyfriend, who was now at Stanford. Might one of us, both of us, come visit?

Ann and I have a ritual on the phone.

"Who's the best girl?" I ask as I'm signing off.

"Me," she says.

"And who loves you the most?"

"*Me.*"

We laugh, and I pass her on to Blair.

Ann must have asked about the weekend. Blair said something about a movie. Ann must have asked which one. I would have named the movie we'd just watched with Jared, but Blair blurted out, "*Y Tu Mamá También.*" And blushed.

CHAPTER 19

What happens in our lives most days is domestic, grooved. If she has no official obligations, Blair walks home from Barnard and does two laps on the reservoir track. A little later I come home and assemble what passes for cocktails and kibbles: wine, fruit, and a chunk of cheese. Blair returns, not even winded, showers, and joins me at the dining room table. We catch up. Have sushi delivered. Separate. Read, work, reconvene, and . . .

But on Monday, I arrived home to find Blair at the dining room table, wine already open.

"A nice surprise," I said, and kissed her.

"A day of surprises," she said.

I hadn't noticed the object in front of her. She turned it over. A simply framed black-and-white, five-by-seven photograph of Jean Coin. A self-portrait in the Avedon style: vivid flesh—bare shoulders and chest, ending at the top swell of her breasts—against a white background. For all the skin, it was a chaste picture; your eye was drawn to her face.

In the lower right corner, in neat handwriting:

For Blair & David, in fond friendship. XXXOX, Jean.

"Well then," I said, and filled my glass. "An intimate photograph by a photographer who never takes pictures of people or allows herself to be photographed."

Blair poured more wine.

"Did you see her?" I asked.

"She left it with the doorman."

"What do you make of it?"

"I don't know," Blair said. "I can't stop looking at it."

"I'd be stunned if that wasn't her intent."

"It makes me feel like there's someone here we might want to know." She considered how that sounded, and added, quickly, "As a person."

"How about as a stalker?"

"David, *please.*" Blair set the photo down. "This is her version of a thank-you note."

"'Here's something to remember me by when you are

old and gray and full of sleep and nodding by the fire.' No, I don't think so."

"You're so cold about her," Blair said.

"I was misquoting Yeats. I thought you'd be impressed."

"You were showing off. What you're basically doing is . . . dismissing her."

"Not at all. I'd like to talk to her. Pick her brain about investing in photography."

"As I said: *cold*. For you, she might as well have been a hooker who met us in a hotel."

This is what happens in a long-running marriage: Your partner not only knows *how* you think but *what*. Last week I would have described Jean Coin as a woman who knew what she wanted, went after it, adjusted to accommodate others, and got most of what she wanted. I admired that. Then.

Now the only difference for me between Jean and the escort who would have done our bidding in a hotel room was that Jean didn't fake her pleasure. In every other way, we were a transaction to her. As she was to us. If she gave me advice about investing in photography, that would also be a transaction.

Blair hadn't made this turn. It seemed she'd made another one. The opposite one.

"When I look at the picture," she said, "I see kindness, and intelligence, and peace. And when I think of a hooker . . ."

The sky darkened. The heavens opened. Tears. Sudden tears.

"Darling . . ." I said, and moved to hold her.

"When I was a kid . . ." More words were in her mouth; Blair just couldn't say them. Time marinated. "When I was a kid . . ." A gulp for air. "I wanted to be a ballet dancer." Another gulp. "I read everything I could find about dance. I remember this piece about a great dancer who didn't think he was as great as his hero. He said, 'Jacques takes one step onstage—just one—and you know who he is. Because he is completely, totally himself.'"

"Blair . . ."

"Jean has that. You can see it. She has it."

"In the picture. You have no idea if—"

"Whatever," she said, beyond arguing the point. "I want that, David. I want it so much. I can't imagine how that would feel. To be myself. Totally, completely myself."

"But you are!"

"I am so far from it! And you know it. Look how I was with Jean. Curious but careful. Open-minded but prim. The good girl. Always the good girl."

"There must be a hundred kids who take you as a model for—"

"In my *job*? I'm *especially* fake there. I never say the blunt, harsh, ugly things when they need to be said. I smooth things over. I'm a vanilla Christian who wants to make it nice for everybody. And I hate that. Just hate it."

Another spasm of sobs. I waited it out.

"I don't see how you do it," she said. "You spend all day dealing with people's problems. The same ones over and over. And you never crack. How do you do it?"

I try not to go there. What's the point? If there were parades for people who suck it up and get on with their lives, the marching would never end.

"I think of the people who depend on me," I said.

"I do too. It's not enough."

"Try thinking about our great good luck."

"What?"

"Do you remember 'Shock and Awe'—the start of the Iraq War?"

"We bombed their cities," Blair said. "Killed thousands of civilians."

I corrected her: "We killed *children*. And cruelty to children . . . I can never understand it, can never hear about it without . . . well, you know . . ."

I had to pause.

"Ann was little then. I used to take her to the playground and watch her swing. Laughing. Shouting. She was just the happiest kid. And I'd look up at the sky . . . blue and empty, with clouds out of a painting . . . and I'd think the same thing every time: The children in Iraq live under this same sky. How does it happen that *my* child is spared? Why don't the bombs drop on *us*? And I know there's no equation that says if I go to work and comfort people who have no idea how . . . *comfortable* they are that she is spared and you are spared, but . . ."

Now it was my turn to choke up.

"I am so sorry about this . . . thing with Jean," I said. "It's all my fault."

"There's no blame here."

"I pushed it. Saturday night never had to happen."

"No. It was good."

A fireball of a sun turned the buildings gold. The last time we'd sat at this table, how playful we were, how happy, how hot. And now we were in another place, where you do something that seems simple and discreet, and it turns out not to be, and you can't get back to where you were. Unintended consequences. The deadliest trap.

What I kept coming back to: This great taboo event was such a small social experiment. A local adventure, two cab rides. How could three hours—not even a night out—have any aftereffect?

*   *   *

Why did Blair have such a high opinion of Jean?

I thought I had the right answer, the answer that sounds smart but doesn't hold up: money.

Blair and I have no trust funds, no inheritance, no seven-figure cushion. We're dependent on income. Always feeling vulnerable, always aware that we're in the upper-middle-class poverty cycle—running on the hamster wheel, no way to escape, flush only until luck fades.

Jean's life was ours but flipped. She was a successful solo act, unburdened by school bills, unworried about loved ones, every day new and rich with possibility. That made Blair—wife, mother, wage slave—feel as if she'd aimed too low, risked too little, achieved nothing great.

If we'd come from money, who could Blair have become? And how much more could I have been? And now, locked into our professional identities as much by fear and inertia as by school bills, how much more could we ever be?

True. All true. And all wrong. Money—Jean's money, our money, the New York obsession with money—was exactly not what Blair was thinking.

"We should get together with Jean again," Blair said.

"Excuse me?"

"Jean. You. Me. Together. One more time."

I felt something in my head that was like nothing I'd ever experienced. If I call it carbonation, that's not quite it. But there was definitely a kind of brain sizzle, like water splashed on a roaring fire. I was speechless, uncomprehending.

Blair waited me out.

"Funny," I said, struggling for a sane, light tone. "I distinctly remember you saying, 'We're not going to make a habit of this.'"

"And we're not. This is it. With Jean. With anybody."

I poured a glass of wine, busying myself like an actor in an antique melodrama.

"Why the change of heart?"

My self-control sounded impressive, but it was a sham. Not that Blair noticed. She didn't need my question—she wanted to talk. Whatever came next had been percolating for some time.

"I wanted to say yes to new things, and this was the first yes," she said. "But I cheated. I didn't commit. I watched Jean. I watched you. And I watched myself watching myself watching myself . . . I did it all wrong. Now I want to get it right."

"Pick something else."

"I'll pick a lot of things. But this first."

"Blair, please . . ."

 "I want to confront this."

"Really?"

"Yes," she said, with complete conviction. "Yes."

CHAPTER 20

Jean entered our apartment as if she lived there.

Relaxed. Self-assured. Clearly pleased that she had achieved, however briefly, a continuing presence in our lives. *Validated*—that's the word. Like she'd made it through the first round of the threesome playoffs.

There was another difference this time. To her natural appeal, Jean added makeup. I wouldn't have imagined she owned any. But she'd applied a thin line of silver at the eyelid and the faintest of pink lipsticks—teenager's makeup. And she'd abandoned her uniform for a T-shirt, thin cardigan sweater, and a short denim skirt—preppy choices. And was that . . . scent? Yes, scent—a light citrus perfume that made me think of women coming off tennis courts in Newport.

Blair wore a white shirt, mostly unbuttoned, and jeans.

Jean's look: a close cousin to what Blair had worn to Jean's loft last week.

Blair's look: more or less what Jean always wore.

They got the joke right away.

"Love your outfit," Blair said.

"Love yours," Jean said.

I got a quick hug from Jean, who moved on to kiss Blair on both cheeks.

And then we stood there, not knowing what to do next. Understandable. Really, what do you say? "A week ago, you were standing by your bed, bent over, me pounding deep into you as you applied your mouth to Blair. And here you are again."

I didn't say that. But I thought it. I'd thought it all week. Two women. Two fascinating women, hot in the best possible way: quietly, privately hot. Tonight that didn't thrill me. I sensed nothing good could come of this.

"Why does this feel . . . weird?" Jean asked.

"Because we're here," I said. "Surrounded by pictures of our family . . . ten feet from the room where we raised our kid."

"Should we go downtown?"

"No," Blair said. "We should drink."

*   *   *

We moved to the dining room, where two bottles waited in an ice bucket. The choice was between a better brand of champagne than we usually drink and an unlabeled bottle of clear liquor with sprigs of rosemary and slices of lemon peel inside.

I lifted the bottle. "This is vodka. Improved by a friend. It's very smooth. Sweet, almost. But dangerously strong."

"You might want champagne," Blair said.

"Vodka," Jean said.

The alcohol content was outrageous, but there was no burn. We knocked back a few shots as Jean murmured compliments about our modest photography collection. When the tour ended, we found ourselves at the living room window, looking out at the park. A romantic view. In other circumstances.

"There's something I have to say."

My first thought: Whatever Jean says, it's one reason we shouldn't be seeing her tonight.

My second thought: And we should cut off all communication with Jean the second she's out the door.

"A little sincerity goes a long way," I cautioned.

"Don't worry, David—it's still sports. But I don't usually have a connection deeper than skin, so it was nice to be with people who had . . . feelings. And that it was mutual? Sweet."

Silence. Of the awkward variety.

"Almost mutual," Blair said. "I'll do better tonight."

Blair reached for Jean and kissed her on the mouth. The kiss was intense. And long.

I watched, rapt, as Blair slipped her hand between Jean's legs, doing to Jean what Jean had done to her last week. Jean gasped, jerked her head back, ending the kiss. But she didn't move Blair's hand away—they were deeply connected. Blair tightened her hand, as if she planned to lift Jean. The effect was powerful. Jean's eyes closed. She arched her back. Her face contorted and her mouth puckered. Breath held, then released. Long sigh. Shake of head. Eyes opening.

"Wow," Jean said, putting a hand on the windowsill to steady herself. "Just . . . wow."

"Sorry, David," Blair said, hugging me. "That had to happen."

Jean raised her hand and made a gentle sweeping motion toward the park below. "The pattern of the lights," she said.

"It's one of the apartment's main attractions," I said.

"A chain of DNA. A distant galaxy." Jean giggled. "Or that old cliché: a string of pearls."

She pointed, dotting the air with her fingers. Was this the photographer talking? Or was she drunk? I know I was; my resistance to Jean had melted. Her arm was suddenly the most beautiful flesh I'd ever seen. I would have followed it anywhere.

I stroked Jean's arm. I licked her fingers.

"Ohmigod," I said. "I am . . . baked."

"I'm more glazed than the window," Blair said, and extended her arm so I could lick her fingers too.

I felt like I was swimming underwater. Every gesture required a decision. Two thoughts were one more than I could handle.

"Anybody else . . . dizzy?" I asked.

Laughter told me we were all in the same condition. "Bed," Blair said.

A decade ago, when the dollar was strong enough for us to go to great European cities out of season, Blair and I spent a Christmas in Venice. We found empty churches, shuttered restaurants, and outrageous sales. On Madison Avenue, we're too intimidated by Frette to go inside. In Venice, at Macy's prices, we bought sheets. As soon as we unpacked in New York, we put them away, on the theory they were too good to use. But on Saturday morning, Blair had washed them in some special soap and put them on the bed. So when we ripped off the comforter, a clean, clothesline, summer-house smell hit us like a snort of cocaine. And now every sense seemed heightened.

Was this sex—or wrestling? Impossible to tell what the goal was, but we all seemed in a hurry to get somewhere. We pushed one another, pulled, slapped. I've never felt more like an animal. Bared teeth were next. Howling wasn't far off.

I could feel Blair's urgency. I moved aside as she wrapped her hands tight on Jean's wrists and started grinding on her.

"You like that?"

Jean was silent.

"Talk to me!"

Jean moaned, writhed, but didn't speak. Blair lowered herself until their faces were inches apart.

"Tell me."

But the time for hot talk was over—Jean was in the throes of a titanic orgasm. She pounded against Blair, shaking her head from side to side.

"Ohmigod," Jean whispered. "Oh, you . . ."

"Yes," Blair hissed. "Oh yes."

"Come with me."

"I will . . . I am," Blair whispered. "Now . . . oh, now . . ."

They convulsed. Collapsed. Only their breathing suggested they were alive.

After a minute, Jean regained this much speech: "Thank you."

"Think nothing of it."

Any words might have sounded funny at this moment, like recovered speech or a line translated from an alien tongue. I would have voted for silence; the beating hearts of Blair and Jean would have been commentary enough. But once someone starts talking . . .

"Think?" Jean put on an Eastern European accent. "What is this thing—*think*?"

Laughter followed, full-throated laughter. It took me by surprise, like a favorite song from the distant past—Blair hadn't laughed like this outside of a movie theater for at least a decade.

"David?" Blair whispered. "You okay?"

No, not exactly. I felt lost and left behind, in a blizzard of emotions—irritation, jealousy, bruised pride—that I knew I couldn't acknowledge.

"Borderline."

"Stay with us."

"Going nowhere."

"Oh, yes, you are," Jean said.

She took me in her hand. Leaned over me, eyes open, as if framing me for a private, interior camera. A century-old camera, requiring a long time exposure—she didn't move, letting the moment fill and ebb and build again. In seconds, I was squirming.

"How do you do that?" Blair asked.

"No secret," Jean said. "You just . . . pay attention." She leaned in. "Very close attention."

She opened her mouth and circled me, again not moving.

I thought about porn movies that show women doing men as if they're going for a world record. Jean knew better—our deepest pleasure comes in the exchange of very delicate information. It happens in the head. Orgasm gets the silver medal.

Eyes closed tight. Slow breathing. Such quiet in the bedroom that we could hear street traffic ten floors below.

Blair got up and started some music. A guitarist from Niger had taken American blues and filtered it through African desert music. His sound was insistent but subtle, just the right match for Jean's mouth work.

Jean sat up. "You go."

Blair took her place. And I almost wept for my good fortune, because I couldn't tell the difference between Blair and Jean.

It got even better. Just like in the porn movies, Blair and Jean took turns working on me. Their mouths were velvet. Their fingers were exquisite torture. I reached out, wanting my hands on flesh, but I was ordered to be still.

And then . . . nothing. I opened my eyes. Blair and Jean were kissing, holding each other tight. Then they found another use for their mouths. While, once again, I watched.

Maybe this is how it works, I thought. Some for me, some for them. Only fair. I was getting the most: two women doing me, every man's dream. But I seemed to have lost the power to influence events. Sparks were crackling between Jean and Blair. Meanwhile, I was being . . . managed.

The second time the women moved away from me, I had the unsettling feeling that I was being . . . excluded. And, once again, I had the feeling that they knew it and didn't care—that's how hot they were for each other. Then, once again, it was as if they knew what I was thinking and made a swift, smooth transition back to me.

This time it was Jean who turned first. But not a Jean I'd seen before. This one sat up in bed, took a bottle of water, poured a thin stream on her shoulders, and rubbed her chest and stomach until she glistened. Then, looking right at me, she struck a pose.

It wasn't a glimpse; it was a display. Jean was putting on a show, giving a private exhibition. And she was a sensational model. She knew how women looked and how photographers get them to look hungrier, hotter. I wouldn't be surprised if she had tried these poses at home, photographed them, and studied them until she was sure she was magic.

Blair moved to her. Jean gently pushed her away.

"Just look," she whispered.

Jean was in no rush. She cupped her breasts, tugged at her nipples. She ran a finger between her legs, gave us the Georgia O'Keeffe view.

I will see those images as long as I live.

I could watch for only so long, and then I pounced.

Blair did too, and after that, it was pure sex. Try this. Try that. So many combinations. We obliterated my checklist.

"Now me," Jean said as she pulled away. "Just me."

She kissed Blair. "May I?"

"With David?"

"It's only this once."

Blair nodded. I pushed into Jean. The contact was electric. I abandoned thought and shed all restraint, and I pushed deeper. Throbbing, I came and came and came.

CHAPTER 21

"Gloomy Sunday." That song was correctly named. Ditto "Stormy Monday." And it had been like that ever since we cheek-kissed Jean out the door on Saturday night. Who annoyed me? Jean. But also Blair. Had they played me? If they hadn't, where did these flashes of rejection and paranoia come from?

Mostly, I was annoyed with myself. I didn't know why, and I knew that I didn't. All I was sure of was that I was spoiling for a fight.

So I had one. With Victoria, of all people. On the very first call of the week.

"Oh, V. I have a small but intriguing piece of gossip," I said as soon as we'd completed the pleasantries. "You know your friend Barbara?"

"The social secretary to—"

I didn't have to name Barbara's employer. He's one of the richest men in the country. When his townhouse was featured in *Architectural Digest*, the liberal columnist in the *Times* wrote that his wife's dressing room was so big it had its own bathroom.

"Exactly."

"Reboot saw her at JFK Thursday night. She was meeting an extravagantly handsome young man, just off the plane from LA. Reboot recognized her, saw that the young man had no suitcase, so he followed them—right to the townhouse."

"It's a very large house," V said.

"And missing an occupant," I said. "The lady of the house is in Paris for the shows. Which suggests—"

V cut me off. "It suggests nothing."

"You know the rumors?"

"I've heard them for years. They're . . . inconclusive. At best."

"They *were* inconclusive. Past tense. Six the next morning, Reboot just happens to be parked outside the townhouse. Guess who comes out? The young man. Into the town car he goes and off to the airport. Reboot follows. But he doesn't need to. He knows the drill—the kid is on the eight a.m. back to LA."

"Coincidence," V said. "Anecdote."

"Exactly," I said. "No record of the event. The wife won't believe this . . . unless, when she comes back from Paris, she sees photos."

I could hear her sigh. "Reboot 'just happened' to be at the house at six a.m.?"

"I gave him no direction."

"He took pictures?"

"Time-stamped."

"What happens next?"

"Nothing," I said. "But if that picture ran on Page Six, the wife might look for a matrimonial lawyer."

"Someone like . . . me?" V asked.

"Who's more respected?"

"I am slightly amazed, David, that you want to move forward here. What's your endgame?"

"A payday. We can bill to the moon."

"I don't need one," V said. "Do you?"

"No. But I'd like one."

In court, V was noted for the brevity of her cross-exams. The extreme brevity: She often asked the one essential question and left the one essential answer echoing in the courtroom. The same in conversation. As now.

"What do you want to buy?" she asked.

Picture a schoolboy caught by a history teacher during

the final exam with the names of the kings of England and their dates written on his shirt cuff.

"Well . . ." Out of the air, I pulled a response: "Art."

"Really." V's tone was vintage Newport. "At what level?"

"Modest. I want to collect photography."

"You could do that now."

"Not quite, V. The world has discovered photography." I knew one fact, and I played it. "A decade ago, Blair and I saw a picture we loved. A Gursky. It cost two hundred and fifty thousand. Which was insane, of course—if we'd had the money, which we didn't, we'd never have spent that. Guess how much that photograph sells for today?"

"A million."

"Two."

Incredulous: "This . . . Gursky . . . this is what you'd like to buy?"

"What I'd like to be doing is *selling* it."

"You know where to find the next Gursky?"

No, I wanted to shout, but Jean Coin does. Blair and I fucked her, and she got more out of it than I did, and she owes me, and she's going to pay me back by selling me some of her pictures without the gallery markup.

"I've met an expert who can advise me."

"Good boy. I am all in favor of seeing you profit tenfold

in a decade. But listen to me. We are talking about a billionaire who dumps toxic waste near poor neighborhoods because he knows to the dollar how light the fines will be. And he knows exactly how much free speech he can buy and what it costs for politicians to make his speech their speech. And, clearly, he knows how to get what he needs in bed without making a ripple."

She paused. I knew she wasn't done.

"And I believe there is something else he knows . . . there is no law for the rich."

"Rich people get divorced," I said. "The law works just fine."

"I'm not talking about his marriage, David. I'm saying this: This man is dangerous. If you get in his way, you have no idea how far he'll go."

"I expect he'll—"

"David . . . *never fuck with people who have more than a billion.*"

Had I ever heard V swear before? No. But I was in a state. I made one last try. "I'd like to pursue this, V. I could drive out . . ."

V laughed. "Oh, David, I do adore you. But this . . . scheme of yours isn't for us. Don't come out here. Don't mention this again on the phone. Don't send me anything electronically. And do give my love to Blair."

CHAPTER 22

Thursday, October 12. The kind of crisp New York day I used to savor, until 9/11 was one of them.

If I had been annoyed on Monday, I was seething by Thursday. Blair and I were talkers, not fighters; there had never been tension at home. Now there was. Blair wouldn't say what was bothering her, and I knew better than to ask.

On Thursday evening, my plan was to retreat to Ann's room and watch the baseball playoffs, which probably wouldn't hold my attention but would at least preserve domestic tranquility.

I didn't see a single pitch.

Blair and I were at the dining room table, eating takeout Pad Thai in a silence heavier than the noodles.

"David," Blair began, and right there, in the first word, I

knew I wasn't going to like whatever came next. This is a legacy of my childhood—in a family that generated nicknames weekly, my mother only called me by my given name when a lecture followed. Blair knew this. But there it was: "David." Followed by: "I have news."

My response was an audible breath.

"Not medical," she said. "It's about us."

She paused.

"What I'm going to say . . . what I'm going to do . . . when I tell you, you'll take it like it's something I'm doing against you. It's not *against* you; it's *for* me. And, I hope, for us."

Another pause.

"I'm going to live with Jean until she leaves for Africa."

"What!"

"It's just six weeks," she said in a nervous rush.

I couldn't help sneering. "*Just* six weeks?"

"I wouldn't be doing this if I didn't know it had an end."

"Please listen to yourself."

"I know," Blair said. "It sounds insane."

"It *is* insane. You don't know this woman at all."

"And I won't know her when it's over."

"What if it's not over when she leaves? You have no certainty there."

"She's leaving. It ends right there."

"Ever heard of Skype?"

"I'm coming back, David. That's a given. She leaves, and that's it. Back to my marriage. Back to you."

"You can't be sure. Jean put her hand between your legs using some code known only to women, and you melted. It might not take forty-one nights for you to be in love with her."

"I grant you, it sounds girlish."

"Our daughter is 'girlish.' As in 'charming.' This is just plain naïve."

"Then think of it as a growth experience."

I could not believe this language.

"'Growth experience' is bullshit," I said. "It's a synonym for *mistake*."

"It's the truth."

"I see only one truth—you're going off to fuck Jean for six weeks."

Blair was the picture of calm.

"Darling, there will be sex. I like to think there will also be *talking*. And . . . *understanding*. And . . . *growth*."

"What next? Birkenstocks? Armpit hair?"

"David, *please*. Talk to me like I'm a finely tuned instrument."

"Say that again. The last part."

As if in an adult education English-as-a-second-language class: "I'm a finely tuned . . ."

"What the fuck, Blair? You don't talk like that. Have you been going to a shrink?"

"I'm not seeing a shrink. I'm not reading self-help books. I didn't join a cult."

At last I understood. "Of course. This is all Jean."

A shrug. The least possible confirmation.

"This took more than a phone call," I said.

"We met."

The narrowest possible admission.

"Sleep with her?"

"No."

"Why not?"

"There was a lot to talk about."

Bitterness and bile. Unable to stop. "I'll just bet."

"I'm not doing this because of two nights and a few conversations. I'm doing it for the self-discovery."

"Oh, *please.*"

"Why don't you take some responsibility here?"

"Me?"

"A very large reason for this, dear David, is you. You started this. You sold it to me. For ten years, you sold it to me. Night after night, in bed, making the case. The softness of two women together, the emotional connection, the heat." She whispered, imitating me, "'Oh, another woman just came into the dressing room, Blair.' 'That woman at the table by the window—she's looking at you, Blair.' 'We're in a crowded elevator, Blair.' Am I making this up?"

"It was . . . a game," I said. "Just talking dirty. We played it together."

"Okay, a game. But a game you loved. Only you left something out."

Sigh. Bracing for the accusation.

"If I bought it, there was no reason to involve you. You talked about threesomes, but it usually came down to two women and you watching. And one more thing . . ."

Saving the worst for last? Without doubt.

"Say we'd done it with a man. If I decided to go off with him for a month, would that make you more jealous than my going off with Jean?"

No need to ponder that. "Of course."

"Exactly. Now consider another outcome. We got together with a woman—let's call her Jean Coin. What if it had happened that *you* made a connection with her? And you wanted to live with her for six weeks. Would you have gone?"

"Of course not."

"Even if you wanted to? Even if you desperately wanted to?"

"No."

"You know that if you didn't, every one of those forty-one nights you'd feel . . . thwarted."

"Sure. And for years to come. So what?"

"When you were fucking me, would you be thinking about Jean? Wishing I were Jean?"

"This isn't fair," I said. "You know I'm addicted to you."

Blair didn't respond. She had a case to make, and she wouldn't be deflected.

"You say you wouldn't go to Jean. I say yes, you would. Because I'd make you."

"You wouldn't be jealous?"

"Six weeks of jealous, for Christ's sake. But I'd swallow that because I believe that when you came back, things would be better between us."

"Well, forgive me—I was unaware anything was wrong."

Blair, fighting off tears, pointed at her face. "Does this look *right* to you?"

I shook my head. I couldn't speak. Blair steadied herself and took my hand.

"David, if we're lucky, we're going to have forty, fifty more years together. Things will . . . happen. Maybe things that make this look like kindergarten. But if we get all rigid on each other . . . if we're too scared to live our *real* lives . . .

we won't make it. That's why I'd push you into Jean's bed. Because what we avoid is what will destroy us."

"What if you go to Jean and you find out that you like her better—or like women better? This is what terrifies me."

"I'm coming back. I swear it. I'm coming back."

I wanted to believe her. But I didn't dare. So I cried. And I knew this would not be the last time.

Blair's tears had passed. She believed. In whatever she was doing with Jean. In us.

"Will we . . . see each other?"

"I don't know. Not at first, I don't think."

"Can we talk?"

"Let's start with email—but don't you write the first one."

What astonishing strength! I had none.

"We will have Thanksgiving, David. Ann will be home, and we will give thanks at this table."

Not a bet I would make. I shook my head.

"And decades from now," Blair continued, "one of us will die in the other's arms—I *know* that. I *love* that. And I love you."

We sat in silence, holding hands. No point in arguing. No point in asking for reasons. No point in trying to understand.

This was happening.

CHAPTER 23

On his first day of a business trip to Berlin, Liam Neeson has a car accident in a taxi. Waking from a coma four days later, he's confused about many things but mostly this: Where is his wife? She must be looking for him. She must be frantic. But she's not. So he goes looking for her. When he finds her, she's at a restaurant with another man. Who is, she says, her husband. And can prove it. She's never seen Liam Neeson before. Could management kindly have him . . . removed?

How could a woman look into her husband's eyes and insist she doesn't know him?

It's only a movie. A well-cast actress delivered her lines flawlessly. And we're hurtled so quickly beyond this plot device that we don't ask why Neeson doesn't just Google himself on his iPhone and show the search results to his wife.

But how could Blair not know me?

And how could Blair say I really don't know her?

This had to be a prank, a mistake, or—why had I not thought of this?—some sort of hormonal imbalance, a sign of imminent menopause.

Those were my first-day reactions to Blair's announcement.

Start again.

Spin the story of the last month the other way.

It's Blair who meets someone. A man. Operating under the terms of our understanding, she wants to bring him home. Into our bed.

A man.

This may sound kinky, but Blair having sex with another man is a fantasy I can handle. It works for me because I'd like to watch. From a distance. Not from the same bed.

It's a very specific voyeurism. Ideally, they'd be hidden from the neck down by a sheet. All I'm interested in is Blair's face, how she reacts as she's being pleasured—the straining, eyes closed tight, the release as he comes or she does, whatever.

Going to bed with Blair and another man is trickier.

I'm pretty sure I could handle it if we were both servicing her. Or if she took turns servicing us. Of less interest is kissing a man, touching him, rubbing against him, his mouth on me or mine on him.

Everything, in short, that thrilled me when Blair and Jean did it.

But fair's fair. If that's what Blair wanted from a threesome, how could I refuse to do for her what she had so graciously done for me?

Now spin the story the other way, all the other way.

If a man and I really connected, I could be the one saying I'd be back in six weeks. And I might be the one saying, as Blair said to me, "Darling, there will be sex. I like to think there will also be talking. And . . . understanding. And . . . growth." Blair might have been the one wondering if I'd make good on my promise to return.

Possible. But really . . . not. Because I can't get past the skin. Do I want to reach for a man's face and rub his unshaven beard? Cleave to a nipple covered with fur?

When I spin the story the other way? It's a nonstarter.

I can see why Blair might believe she had a grievance.

CHAPTER 24

Blair left while I was out. She took one suitcase and a hanging bag. I was so numb that her physical absence barely registered.

There's a way to get through setbacks like this:

Don't open your lover's closet and bury your face in an old shirt.

Don't make a mix tape for her.

Don't wait on the steps of her new home "just to say hi."

Don't start drinking Jack Daniel's.

Don't stop shaving.

Don't register with a website that promises to hook you up with women who want more sex than their husbands provide.

Don't eat in front of the refrigerator with the door open. Or out of a can.

If you don't worship, don't start.

Keep your pants on. Once you start walking around the house in boxers, you're on the slippery slope.

For that matter, keep your hands off yourself.

Honor the truths of Little Red Riding Hood: Don't talk to strangers. Stay on the path.

And specifically—I'm talking to myself *now—look on the bright side. Six weeks is not forever. Over the lifespan of a marriage, it's not even a blip; it's exactly as long as a summer enrichment program.*

All those years of wanting to read Tolstoy? Do it now.

Or pick something you're curious about—British rock, 1963 to 1967—and spend nights on the web pulling up links, making your own greatest hits playlist.

Buy teeth-whitening strips and faithfully apply them.

It's easier to move steel than people; step up your exercise routine.

Feel the need for a social life? Volunteer at a soup kitchen.

What about your friends? Don't see them. Exceptions: If they're in the hospital, have just lost a job, or are imminently moving to a distant city—if they're worse off than you.

Go to every movie in the Eisenstein retrospective at MOMA.

Slippage is natural. You will backslide. So cut yourself some slack. Think of it as going off your diet on Saturday night.

Do you have a sudden, unhealthy fascination you want to research? Here's a card entitling you to one free night of wallowing.

I had one of those sick fascinations: whether three people can fit in one relationship. So I launched a research project. Didn't wait for Saturday.

This was my question: Is a triangle a legitimate relationship for three strong, emotionally mature people?

I didn't ask about threesomes or romantic triangles—I

knew what I'd get. I just typed in *triangles*. Soon I learned how the triangle is the strongest shape in nature. And how, in the 1930s, Buckminster Fuller invented the geodesic dome, which is made of triangular panels fitted together.

Geodesic domes can be thrown up quickly and inexpensively. Which the government did, in weather stations in Alaska and the South Pole. Which hippies did, in the late sixties, in New Mexico and Colorado. Those regions have something in common: horrendous storms. But storms don't wreck domes, even hippie farm domes made from chopped-up car roofs. Clearly, something about the strength of the triangle makes the geodesic dome resist gale-force winds.

Or consider the "triangle offense" that was so successful for Phil Jackson when he coached the Chicago Bulls and the Los Angeles Lakers. Critics dismissed it as rigid and archaic. Jackson saw it as a flexible structure that encouraged superstars to play as a team and be creative. "When the triangle is working right, it's virtually impossible to stop it," Jackson wrote, "because no one knows what's going to happen next, not even the players themselves." And what is "working right"? Every player engaged. All the players moving together.

Inevitably, the question became this: If the triangle is the strongest shape in nature and the most successful formation in sports, why isn't it the strongest form of human relationships?

Because it just isn't. As kids sent to multichild playdates know, three invariably splinters into two and one. And even if the idea had merit, it wouldn't matter—Blair and Jean were not begging me to move in with them.

Or even sending the occasional "hope you're okay" email.

CHAPTER 25

When an animal in the woods gets sick, it goes deeper into the woods, burrows in, and sleeps. It stays asleep, as much as possible, until healed. With Blair gone, I followed animal wisdom: Lay low, keep quiet.

So in October, all my nights were one night, the same night. The dining room was my default location. A goose-neck lamp cast a pool of light as I typed on a laptop. Mozart horn concertos suggested order. And there was order: no open Chinese restaurant takeout boxes, no pyramid of empty beer cans, no ashtray overflowing with cigar stubs.

In other circumstances, this might be a picture of a man in the throes of creative effort. Sadly, this is a picture of a man churning out emails that couldn't be sent:

Blair—I know we said you'd contact me first . . .

Blair—Shouldn't have looked through the photo albums, but . . .

Blair—So I went to the Met. And there did see a painting . . .

Blair—"If equal affection cannot be," Auden wrote . . .

Oh, Blair, sweet Blair, I . . .

Unproductive then and embarrassing now. In my defense, when I wrote these blasts, I thought I'd print them out and bind them—a record of a sad season. To be shared with Blair or not, depending.

On the plus side, I ran in the morning and again at night. I took on a pro bono case—a mother of two married to such a monster that a protection order wasn't sufficient and I had to move her to another city. I opened more doors for the infirm and elderly, was more generous in my thanks for services, noticed the city's castoffs and peeled off dollar bill after dollar bill.

Along the way, I achieved a modest balance. I wasn't a man who pimped his wife, a man unworthy of love. There had been more hands than just mine on the tiller. Blame was a luxury. A postmortem had no point. Survival was victory. I had twinges, but most of the time, I wasn't beating myself up.

La Rochefoucauld: "No man can look long upon the sun or death."

In late October, I labored to be his Exhibit A.

CHAPTER 26

But I regressed.

She called herself Madame Bovary. I hadn't read the novel in decades, but I remembered the carriage ride, curtains down, Bovary and her lover scandalously having at it.

There were many other Manhattan women on the cheaters' website. Their pseudonyms were more to the point: ChasteOne, 38Dee, CumHere. Madame Bovary was the only name that suggested this woman had read a book between trysts. That affinity sufficed.

Using the confidential messaging form on the cheaters' site, I gave myself the name of a lawyer who became a best-selling author—John Grisham—and began a conversation:

JOHN GRISHAM: *In the novel, she kills herself. When you chose the name, did you think of that?*

MADAME BOVARY: *Of course. She dies alone. No worries for you.*

JOHN GRISHAM: *I don't wish to contribute to your demise.*

MADAME BOVARY: *Don't flatter yourself. There were others before you. There will be more after.*

JOHN GRISHAM: *Who are you?*

MADAME BOVARY: *Your mirror. Married, not happily.*

JOHN GRISHAM: *I'm happily married.*

MADAME BOVARY: *Please.*

JOHN GRISHAM: *Happily married with a temporary bump.*

MADAME BOVARY: *Never done this before, I see.*

JOHN GRISHAM: *How can you tell?*

MADAME BOVARY: *The clichés. Repeaters are slicker. Funnier.*

JOHN GRISHAM: *So I'm green. School me.*

MADAME BOVARY: *Height. Weight. Age. Income.*

JOHN GRISHAM: *5'9". 175. 46. None of your business. Who are you?*

MADAME BOVARY: *A woman who'd respond to a guy who calls himself John Grisham. Whom I admire. He's our Dickens.*

JOHN GRISHAM: *You write?*

MADAME BOVARY: *Between patients. I'm a psychiatrist.*

JOHN GRISHAM: *What brings you here?*

MADAME BOVARY: *I'm looking for a lover who knows enough to do one thing slowly. Know what I mean?*

JOHN GRISHAM: *Yes. If you do that, it feels like the energy . . . builds.*

MADAME BOVARY: *Exactly. So I like him to start with his hand between my legs. And just . . . hold it.*

JOHN GRISHAM: *I do that.*

MADAME BOVARY: *And then I like it when he puts his arm there.*

JOHN GRISHAM: *I can do that.*

MADAME BOVARY: *And then I like the tip of his tongue just touching me.*

JOHN GRISHAM: *Emma, what do you look like?*

MADAME BOVARY: *Under oath, Mr. Grisham? For 50, I'm hot.*

JOHN GRISHAM: *I'd like specifics.*

MADAME BOVARY: *Standard Hotel. Tomorrow. 5:30 p.m. Ask for Bovary.*

JOHN GRISHAM: *Isn't that the hotel where couples leave the curtains open so people on the High Line can watch them?*

MADAME BOVARY: *It is. And if you're willing to do it in the window, I'll let you have my ass.*

Those words stopped me. As a sentence—words in combination—and as an idea. A wall of windows. A woman, standing parallel to the window, leaning over. A man, lubricated, slipping inside. The woman, breathing into the pain. Or welcoming it. The warmth. The tightness.

Bovary knew exactly what the pause in my typing meant.

MADAME BOVARY: *I'm talking about the thing your wife*

doesn't let you do, am I right? Or she did before you got married but won't now. The thing you most want . . .

JOHN GRISHAM: *Emma, you're out of my league. I'm sorry.*

I left the cheaters' site. Didn't return. In this world, I'm an amateur, and glad about it.

CHAPTER 27

A key turned. The front door opened. I switched from my evening ritual—unsent email to Blair—to a law blog I kept open in hopeful anticipation of this very moment. I pretended to be absorbed. I rehearsed surprise.

"Daddy!"

I was instantly laid low. And, just as fast, revived. Ann is the daughter every parent dreams of and we got. Colic as an infant and no trouble after that. Really, none. Great grades, good at sports, author of alternately funny and outraged editorials in the school paper. She's in the center of every class picture. She's the one reaching out to the new scholarship kids from the Bronx. The food drive at Thanksgiving, the soup kitchen not just at Christmas, building a house in Haiti in the blast furnace of summer—that's Ann.

Ann is beautiful but doesn't grasp it, and if anyone insists that she is, she's confused—she understands beauty to be about cosmetics, and she uses none. There's her mother's brightness and curiosity in the eyes, her mother's skin, her mother's effortless athleticism. Like her mother, Ann's clothes—jeans, a sweater, J.Crew barn jacket—are cared for but not fussed over.

Her mother's child.

A whirl of motion. I jumped up, she dropped her backpack, we hugged, I pulled away to look at her, she grabbed me again, and we stood that way for some time, two hearts beating fast.

"I had to come," she whispered.

"Why?" I asked, though I knew the answer.

"I talked to Mom."

"What did she say?"

"That you're taking a break until Thanksgiving."

"We are."

"That seemed strange."

"What?"

"That she'd move out. What happened?"

"Something small and stupid and all my fault."

"I can believe that," Ann said.

I realized I'd been holding on to my daughter literally "for dear life." I liberated her, weak with relief—Blair hadn't told Ann about the threesome and what it had led to. And she wouldn't. Whatever we'd done to each other, we wouldn't spill the damage into Ann's life.

I couldn't say what, but there was something different about Ann now, something acquired at college in two short months. How could that have happened? You watch her change and chart her growth for eighteen years, and suddenly she's left home, and you're not sure you shouldn't introduce yourself and start over.

"Hungry?" I asked.

"I had something on the train."

"I'd love an omelet. You?"

She nodded, and we moved to the kitchen.

"You look . . . great," I said, as I busied myself with eggs and cheese.

"You too," she said, a little too quickly.

"One of us is lying."

Before I made the omelets, I reached for the coffee grinder and beans.

"Could I have hot chocolate?" Ann asked.

A small surprise. Ann is, like me, a coffee snob.

"I haven't seen you drink hot chocolate since that snowstorm," I said, foraging in the cabinet. "How long ago was that?"

"I was fourteen. We walked in the park all the way to the Boathouse."

"We sat at the bar. You thought you were so big."

"What a joke," Ann said. "The waitress wore a white blouse and a black bra, and I said she must be French. And you agreed."

"She wasn't?"

"Brooklyn." She punched me. "As you remember."

"I loved walking with you in that storm," I said. "But really, what *don't* I love about you?"

"The perks of an only child."

We talked about Tufts and her courses and why she wasn't running cross-country and how studying international relations and diplomacy was like splitting the difference between her father, who gets warring parties permanently separated, and her mother, who builds relationships. We talked about her high school friends and how they were adjusting to college. We kicked some politicians around, and she brought me up-to-date on new music.

Then it was late. One more thing to say. I'd been avoiding it.

"About Thanksgiving. If you want to bring someone home and are now thinking maybe that's not a good idea . . . it's a good idea."

"Waifs and strays?" Ann asked.

"All your loser friends."

In the movie version, Ann pretends to wince at my bad, old joke, punches me and hugs me, and goes to her room to play music too loud. And in the final shot of that scene, as good old dad starts to wash the dishes, he smiles, as if to say: I am halfway to okay.

In real life, Ann dropped the mask.

First, the setup. "If I bring my friends home, how do I know it won't be *Who's Afraid of Virginia Woolf*?"

"Your mother and I are fine," I said. "This is just a . . . moment."

Now the knife: "Why was Mom choked-up on the phone?"

There was nothing I could say.

The first thrust: "If your dog was in that kind of pain, you'd put it down!"

"We're not . . . in touch," I said. "I didn't know."

"You didn't know you hurt her?"

"I do know that."

"What did she ever do to you? *What?*"

If I could have said anything, it would have been something like . . . well, I don't know. How do you tell your daughter you're sorry for what you and her mother did in bed?

CHAPTER 28

And on the 22nd day . . . Blair sent me a midafternoon instant message. I had to smile; instant messaging is archaic. Who uses instant messages these days? Older people, when they need to communicate more than location and mood and when their kids aren't around to mock them.

BLAIR: *I hurt. I'm not blaming you. As they say: "No victims, only volunteers." I didn't see that for so long. Now I do. Not that I'm "a finely tuned instrument"—forgive me for that. When I said it, I was in crazy pain. I'm better now. I acknowledge my complicity. Boy, do I have work to do. And so do you, because, over years, small, persistent wrongs have a cumulative effect: blunt force trauma. And I love you.*

A first-draft, top-of-the-head blast? Not close. It had the force of weeks of thought. But it called for an immediate response.

ME: *Pleased to hear from you. Can we talk?*

BLAIR: *Not today. Your voice would unnerve me.*

ME: *We could meet. Wear dark shades. Pass notes.*

BLAIR: *To what point?*

ME: *Broker a peace treaty. Discuss our child. Or make out under the bleachers. Whichever comes first.*

BLAIR: *You'll be pleased to know I rapped Ann's knuckles.*

ME: *She's just a kid.*

BLAIR: *This isn't her business. She's being a moralizing little brat. And she's rewriting family history—remember, in the Bahamas, when Kenny Klein was driving the boat, and he went faster and faster?*

ME: *Ann was scared. I asked him to slow down.*

BLAIR: *And Kenny said, "She's got a life vest. Even if I flip the boat, she'll be alright." Ann sobbed and sobbed. You grabbed the wheel and stopped the boat.*

ME: *He never talked to me again.*

BLAIR: *Ann now tells it like she got hysterical and Kenny stopped only because she begged him.*

ME: *Weak, irresponsible dad.*

BLAIR: *Who never put her arm around her. Who never told her she was safe as long as you were in this world.*

ME: *Doesn't matter.*

BLAIR: *It does. Whatever our differences, you're a great dad.*

ME: *Thanks. Right now I only care about getting my wife's chin off the table.*

BLAIR (ignoring me): *I've got to return to my regular scheduled programming.*

ME: *Will you think I'm "controlling" if I suggest a book?*

BLAIR: *Sigh.*

ME: When Things Fall Apart, *by Pema Chödrön.*

BLAIR: *Can you just summarize his message?*

ME: Her *message.*

BLAIR: *A female writer. How like you.*

ME: *I'm ignoring that. Here's a story she tells: A poor family had a son they loved beyond measure. He was thrown from a horse and crippled. Two weeks later, the army came to the village and took every able-bodied man to fight in the war. The young man was allowed to stay behind with his family.*

BLAIR: *So?*

ME: *For Pema Chödrön, that's the moral: "Life is like that. We call something bad; we call it good. But really we just don't know."*

BLAIR (after ten seconds of silence): *Well, that's where I'm at. I don't* know.

ME: *I'm there too.*

CHAPTER 29

"Well, look at the bronze goddess!" I said, with a lightness that anyone else might have believed.

Victoria didn't. And didn't pretend to. So I didn't try to divert her with questions about what she'd been reading as she spent her afternoons wrapped in a blanket on a chaise on her lawn at the beach.

"How are you, David?"

"Fine. What brings you to town, V?"

"When they harvest the pumpkins, it's time."

"Coffee?"

"I'll get it later. May I sit?"

I stood, thinking we'd take the couch. But she sat across the desk, like a client, which told me everything. If a hole appeared in the floor before me, even a hole leading somewhere deep and dark and crawling with snakes at the bottom, I would have jumped in.

"I'm okay, V," I said. "Really. You don't have to worry about—"

"When someone is *worried*, David, it's usually too late. I am . . . *concerned*."

"Why?"

"I talked to Blair," she said. And, anticipating my question, she quickly added, "I called her."

"Why?"

"Intuition."

"She may have exaggerated what happened. It's not that heavy."

There was kindness in V's voice. "There's nothing heavier than a broken heart."

I knew then what it would be like to get a late-night phone call from the police.

V paused. She seemed to be fighting off an unruly idea, then gathered herself. "Let me speak first as a lawyer—as *your* lawyer. You and Blair had a verbal contract, binding for both of you: 'If you're going to stray, bring that person home.'"

I blushed. I cringed. For Victoria, having to utter a sentence like that . . .

"Blair broke that agreement by not consulting you on the question of her moving out and living with . . ."

"Jean Coin."

"Thank you. Given the care you took, over several years, to craft your original agreement, what Blair did was casual and reckless. She damaged the agreement and—much worse—she damaged your relationship."

"She had some help," I said. "Agreeing to see Jean a second time—that was my fault."

"I was getting to that. You, as a lawyer, should have seen that a second encounter would establish a budding relationship—the very situation the contract was created to avoid. But you're lucky. Every day there are wives who leave their husbands for other women and never come back. Blair is coming home."

V sat back and pressed a hand to her head. She looked her age and then some.

"Are you okay?" I asked.

"Water, please."

I got a bottle from the side table and poured a glass. No ladylike sip for V—she gulped it down.

"Blair is coming home," V said. "But not to the same marriage. She's different. You're different. You can't start over. You have to be where you are—wherever you are."

V stood and faced me. She gestured for me to stand and come to her, and when I did, she put her hands on my shoulders. Looking at us, you'd think we were about to dance. But the image I had was of a very wise elder, near the end of her life, passing on the core truths.

"There is one thing you must do to rescue your marriage," V said, her eyes locked on mine. "And that is to pretend none of this ever happened. Don't ask Blair any questions. Make no references to . . . that woman."

"What if Blair—"

"Don't pick up the rope."

"I don't know what that means."

"If Blair brings it up, you can't respond with a smart remark. You can't disagree with her about it. You cannot have thirty seconds of dialogue about this . . . episode. If you must, make a brief apology, but say nothing more. It's this simple: Don't . . . pick . . . up . . . the rope. Because there is always someone at the other end. And once you have the rope in your hand, you're in a tug-of-war. And you'll lose. Even if you win, you'll lose."

"Very difficult."

"All but impossible," V said. "But nothing else works."

"I'll do anything that makes the pain go away."

"I remember when my marriage ended, it was horrible. I was in the throes of such pure emotion, it was so . . . raw."

"Yeah," I said. "That's it."

"But I was also strangely happy. It was *good* to feel something so raw. I was completely alive. Any of that happening in you?"

I hadn't considered the utility of pain, the glory of it.

"You're completely alive right now, David. It's rare and enviable. If you and Blair trade it for comfort, you're damn fools."

CHAPTER 30

On October 26, in the middle of the night, Blair sent her first email:

FROM: *Blair.Watkins@gmail.com*
TO: *David@DGLaw.com*
SUBJECT: *Overnight Lows*

D—

I read that book by your friend Pema Chödrön.

I very much liked a story about the Native American grandfather who was speaking to his grandson about violence and cruelty in the world and how it comes about. He said it was as if two wolves were fighting in his heart.

One wolf was vengeful and angry, and the other wolf

was understanding and kind. The young man asked his grandfather which wolf would win the fight in his heart. And the grandfather answered, "The one that wins will be the one I choose to feed."

I am choosing to feed our marriage.

I'm having a hard time.

Bear with me.

CHAPTER 31

As a child, I wasn't ambitious; I was driven. The striving to do well in public school led to the scholarship to a private school. Once there, I moved faster. Always a hand raised in class, fast, like it was a quiz show and you won prizes for knowledge. I minored in after-school activities, piling up lines in the yearbook. The track team—sprinting events, of course. From fourteen on, summer jobs. And, always, clean shirts and neat hair and good manners.

At the same time, the little achiever was completely fixated on girls. Not good enough in sports for the beauty queens. Not musical, so no chance with the rebels in leotards. But I had a mouth, and I used it to debate, to edit the paper, to win small parts in the school plays. There are girls who like that boy, and if he is shrewd enough to ask them what they think and willing to spend the evening listening to them talk, his mouth will be rewarded.

What I learned in Shakespeare class: The hero is highly verbal and highly sexed.

Good deal. Happy to be that hero.

And now I'm not.

I can't make it right.

I've been silenced.

So I read. Too much. The sentences blurred. But there was a Seamus Heaney poem—he said it was one of his favorites—that I read again and again.

The title of the poem is "The Underground." That's the London subway, of course. It's also a reference to the Orpheus myth. A snake bites his wife, and she dies. Broken by grief, Orpheus goes to the Underworld to rescue her. Hard-hearted Hades hears his music and tells him: "You can have her, but if you look back before you're in the upper world, you will lose her forever." Just before they reach safety, Orpheus can't resist—he looks back.

In Heaney's poem, he and his wife are in London on their honeymoon. They're in the subway, late for a concert. She's running ahead of him, buttons popping off her coat, and he follows, like Hansel in the fairy tale, collecting the buttons.

MARRIED SEX

This is how the poem ends:

I come as Hansel came on the moonlit stones
Retracing the path back, lifting the buttons
To end up in a draughty lamplit station
After the trains have gone, the wet track
Bared and tensed as I am, all attention
For your step following and damned if I look back.

When Heaney taught at Harvard, his wife stayed in Ireland, raising their children. He flew home every six weeks. A good husband, a smart man—no scandal is attached to his name.

Seamus and Marie Heaney were married for forty-eight years.

Damned if I'll look back.

CHAPTER 32

Blair never changes her password: our daughter's name and date of birth. I hacked into her Barnard account, saw she had no morning appointments, and headed uptown. Only at her office door did I falter. Blair's decrees versus my need to talk to her: Think, or act? Confront and correct, or let it be?

In one motion, I knocked and entered.

Blair looked up. Not horrified. Not pleased. Stunned. Paralyzed.

"So I was in the neighborhood . . ." I said, and the line came out just as light and frothy as it did when I rehearsed it.

"You broke the rule. You're a . . . *violator.*"

"I throw myself on the mercy of the court."

"My, we are . . . jaunty for a man who's misplaced his wife."

"I'm guided by an old blues line," I said. "*My woman's gone but I don't worry, 'cause I'm sitting on top of the world.*"

When I scripted this conversation, Blair responded with something that would have led to more banter. And in my script, we'd continue playing verbal tennis until I said, "What the fuck are we doing? Let's call it Thanksgiving and break out the champagne," or she said, "You big lug, get over here and kiss me." But I'd apparently worn out what little welcome was available—Blair transitioned to a look of exasperation, the kind seen often in television commercials that depict husbands as well-meaning idiots: Men! Whadya gonna do with them!

"May I?"

Not waiting for an answer, I took the visitor's seat. And—I couldn't help it—gawked.

Blair at her desk, with a cardigan thrown over a buttoned-up blouse. My idea of a centerfold—well, if there were a magazine called *Smart*. There are many more conventionally beautiful women, but Blair has that rare appeal: alertness, a shine in the eye, what my mother would call "sparkle." This is why, when we met, it wasn't difficult to pry Blair from her boyfriend. He didn't really care what she thought, read, wondered about. I did. I still do—all these years later, as much as Blair now seems to think that all I want to do is fuck her, I believe that's a distant second to wanting to lean over and press my head to hers, as if I could download her clarity.

The phone rang. Blair never had her ears pierced, so every phone call during business hours requires her to pluck a pearl clip-on from her right ear and set it on the desk. A gesture out of a 1930s movie. Intoxicating.

"Give me . . . ten minutes," she said, and hung up.

"You look great," I said. "As ever."

Blair was having none of that. "Why are you here?"

"Ten minutes?"

"What, exactly, have you come here to say?" And she checked the time. She wasn't kidding. So be it.

I had an appeal both emotional and logical scribbled as talking points on a card in my pocket. I couldn't remember a word I'd written. My head was as empty as a banker's conscience.

"I am not making sense of the world," I said, and then I lost it. "Things are out of control, except for the husbands of my clients, who have so much money they have—in their offices, anyway—the illusion of control, though of course if their personal lives were in control, I'd know about them only by reading about them in the business section, but of course their relationships are ridiculous and insane and in no way in anybody's control . . . and I—know-it-all lawyer who sees the absurdity of their lives so clearly and is nothing but wise about relationships—am living alone, ankle-deep in terror, and . . ."

"David, you're *babbling*!"

Was I? Apparently. And on the verge of veering further out of control.

Blair sat back. This short play performed for an audience of one was pushing her into herself. At any moment, she could withdraw from personal involvement and watch me as a critic.

I pressed my fingertips to my eyes. What did I see in the darkness? Random moments, a mash-up of people, in no chartable sequence. Clients. Blair and Ann. Childhood moments. And then faded, then brighter, an image of V, motherly, serene. Her voice, from afar, words I'd never heard her say: "You are loved more than you can ever know." And I believed I was.

Precious seconds passed. I didn't care. I could say almost everything in a minute.

"Sorry. Just not used to being in a room with you," I said. "Let me do this as a lawyer. One, I do wish to lose myself when I'm in bed with you, but forgive me, I thought that was the point, and not just for me. Two, I know you think the world's biggest drug problem is testosterone—and I agree; I make my living fighting it—but I am not some testosterone-crazed sex addict. Some women want houses and diamonds hanging on the Christmas tree—that's not you. So I've given you what I can. What I thought you valued. Myself. And one of the best ways to give myself to you—to show you how much I love you—is sex. Maybe I didn't present that love in the best form, maybe I've tracked you like a bloodhound, but I've held nothing back. How many husbands can say that? Three, I am feeling like shit. You are too. Shouldn't that tell you that we are deeply in love? And that we can work this out?"

Silence. Then Blair, in a whisper: "Please go."

A knock at the door. "Dean Watkins?"

"Just a minute," Blair called out.

"I thought we had more time," I said.

"No, you thought you'd make me as miserable as you are."

"Sorry if I hit a nerve," I said.

From outside the door: "Dean Watkins, I can come back . . ."

Blair scribbled a note and pushed it across the desk: *5:00.*

I pocketed it without looking at it. Whatever worked for her.

The young woman outside Blair's door was texting

madly. I wanted to tell her that her problems were the inconsequential troubles of youth and not worthy of the dean's attention, but she had a fresh face and a smile off a cereal box, and I saw laughter in Blair's immediate future. And I felt alone beyond alone.

CHAPTER 33

Cold. Drizzle. Dusk at four thirty. In my head: the Mamas and the Papas singing about New York's brown leaves and gray skies and how much better it is in Los Angeles.

Walking from the subway, I turned up my collar. Even on a bleak afternoon, it was so much more exotic in Morningside Heights than on Central Park West. A rainbow neighborhood: college kids from everywhere, women in burkas, the occasional public intellectual. The plaque on an apartment building announcing that Gershwin wrote "Rhapsody in Blue" there. The crowlike cries of the peacocks from the grounds of the Cathedral of St. John the Divine. A bistro across from the cathedral—a film crew could cheat and call this Paris.

And the cathedral. An old haunt, a memory factory. Two

decades ago, when I was broke at the end of the month, Blair and I went there often to hear choirs before going across the street for pizza.

The cathedral is the world's fourth-largest Christian church. From the doors to the altar, it's six hundred and one feet—as they say, two football fields and a football. You can sit and watch someone pray from a distance, and she won't even know you're there.

Funny what you think about when you're watching your wife on her knees in prayer.

I am a lapsed Jew, son of a clan that has total allegiance to Israel, less to a synagogue. Eight nights of presents happened in our home, but not fasting or two sets of dishes. With the Greenfields, achievement trumps faith. And there I'm golden: In three generations, I took us from shtetl to summa. Then this Nice Jewish Boy made it to Manhattan, made a career, made a name, made money. And made a marriage. To a shiksa, of course. My parents forgave this; the birth of the golden grandchild washes away all sins.

Blair comes from church people. Her father passes the collection plate; her mother cooks for the homeless. Dean and Deaconess Watkins raised their kids in the church and in the groups the church sponsored. Choir, Girl Scouts, candy stripers—all the good-girl check marks. It was inevitable that Blair would trade Iowa for New York and marry a Jew. It was equally unsurprising that she'd go to church when she felt the need.

What does she pray for? I used to ask her. She'd never say. In the cathedral, I'd guess she was praying for guidance, declaring herself clueless to her god. That stiff spine in her office? An act of bravery, Little Big Girl stamping her feet, fooling no one. Here, in a sacred space, Blair was a supplicant, not a princess.

If I knew how to pray, I know what I'd pray for: Blair. The terms wouldn't matter. Only the homecoming. But I was too agitated to pray, so I moved a few rows closer and watched Blair.

Could the most beautiful woman in the world be a woman in prayer?

For a few years, for some stupid reason I no longer remember, Blair and I didn't celebrate our birthdays. One frigid birthday night, I felt the absence of joy, and because it was a Friday and the Met was open late, we walked across the park. Nearing Fifth Avenue, we enacted our ritual: a few puffs and then, like communion wafers, breath mints.

We often joked: birthday in Paris. We've never made it. So we'd go to the rooms of nineteenth-century French paintings and pinball around until one grabbed us. Blair was partial to Monet's cathedrals. Summer heat shimmered in those pictures, stone seemed not quite solid—there was more going on here than admiration for the buildings. I was partial to Manet. Not for the nude women—what shocked Parisians in the 1860s wouldn't get a second glance from a sixth grader now. I liked his portraits—women and children on the balconies of their apartments, his family in the garden.

Neither of us knew that Manet had made a series of religious paintings. We'd spent hours in this room, but we'd never noticed his *Dead Christ with Angels*. That birthday night, buzzing, we did.

In this painting, Jesus has a halo, but it's small and faint. He isn't the son of God—this Christ is a dead man. The wound and the stigmata couldn't be more real. You know that Jesus bled, that the blood had congealed, that the blood had crusted.

I'd never considered a mortal Christ. I don't think Blair had either. So the painting rocked us. Blair especially. "All my life I've been told, 'He died for us,'" she said, "but I always moved beyond that, to the rock being rolled back and the Easter eggs and the joy. The death part was just preamble. And here . . . here, it's everything."

In Manet's painting, two angels mourn Jesus, and they

see what we do: a corpse. There's no hope of resurrection. As I sat in the cathedral, I knew why I'd flashed on that painting: I expected to feel what the angels did. But there was no agony on Blair's face. Whatever she'd been looking for, she'd found. The morning's tension had been replaced by serenity. She was breathing in, breathing out, waiting for me.

I walked to her row and took a seat beside her. She didn't look up, but she took my hand, resting her fingers on my wrist. And there we sat, for several minutes, her knowing how she felt, me in the dark but not caring, not worried, because my life had funneled into this moment, this amazing woman tuned to my pulse.

Blair took her hand away and stood, buttoning her coat. I followed her out of the church. The rain had stopped. Leaves were pasted on the street. The lights made Amsterdam Avenue look like a set for a commercial.

"Pizza?"

"Too nostalgic."

"Beer?"

"One."

CHAPTER 34

The bar on the corner was a student hangout. Clever notices in the window. Formica tables. Scarred chairs. It was early, so no students were playing electronic games or shooting pool. There was no waitress. I carried beers. The peace I'd felt in the cathedral had passed; my hands shook.

Fifty blocks and a million light-years from Per Se, here was our past, coming around again.

"So," I said.

My king's pawn.

"So."

Her queen's pawn.

I asked for this meeting. Mine to begin it.

"Doesn't this feel like a first date?"

"Worse," Blair said. "Like we were fixed up."

"Funny. I'm sure I've seen you naked."

"Just that one time."

Two could play this. And two had, often, over the years.

"How was it?" I asked.

"Memorable."

"We should do it again."

"We should."

"How about tonight?"

"David . . . please. We can't joke our way out of this."

Chastened, I nodded.

"Something has become clear to me about us. Our marriage feels intense because we have this fierce romance, but we're skating. We live on the surface. We never fight. We're the envy of everyone we know—the happy-all-the-time Greenfields—but then Jean comes along, and . . . well, you know."

We turn away from intimacy? Hide from each other? I didn't see it.

"And it's not just in our marriage, David—it's in our work. I spend my days in a cloister."

Not an admission I'd ever heard Blair make. But it was the truth. A decade and change ago, when the Internet was in full roar, Blair decided she'd had enough of eighty-hour weeks at

Goldman and took a job at Yahoo. It came with a rich package: big salary, stock options, and the promise of a steady ascent. In a year, she was a vice president. One morning, out of the blue, she was ordered to fire four people. No reason was given, but Blair understood right away that the selection wasn't random. These were her most senior, oldest, highest-paid staffers. The Internet bubble was bursting, so the company needed to run lean. Blair agonized but didn't protest—she had that foursome off the premises by noon. And then, near day's end, someone from human resources showed up and fired Blair.

At that point, she could have found a job in a company run by decent people. She didn't. And now it seemed that she was a lifer at Barnard.

"And you, David . . . you always try to represent wives. You keep your distance from the world of men."

"Correction: the world of power."

"Men," she repeated. "Men freak you out."

Was this so? This was a new idea. I needed to think about it.

"Look at me, David."

I did as instructed.

"There's one more thing we need to get right—the sex thing."

She owned the moment. I kept silent.

"When we started going out, you told me a story. In college, there was a girl who didn't want to date you, just sleep with you—a perfect relationship when you're twenty. One night you took some kind of drug together. I remember your words: 'Our orgasm was alchemy. One moment we were locked together, then we became a single being, and then . . . poof! No bodies, no names. We had disappeared.'"

"Your memory is scary."

"Well, you're a quotable guy. My point . . ." Long pause. "Those things we've done in bed lo these twenty years? I now feel you did them for you. Yeah, you want me to come, and come big, but it's so my orgasm obliterates you. Sex *isn't* connection for you. It doesn't bring you closer; it takes you away."

Another new idea.

"You might ask yourself if someone or something hurt you very badly before I came along. Or if being alive is so painful for you that sex—and only sex—offers a safe way out."

Painful? More painful than this? Not possible. Then that feeling passed, and I felt . . . exposed. What Blair had put out there wasn't pretty, but it was plausible—no, it was probably true.

Sex is my refuge. But for all the years of our marriage,

that wasn't an admission of guilt; it was a badge of pride. I've never once felt I needed to stand up in a church basement and announce, "I'm David, and I'm addicted to sex." That just wasn't our story. I liked sex, and Blair liked sex, so we had sex, a lot of sex. I thought we were, compared to so many, the lucky ones. What I hadn't grasped: In marriage, good sex is a gateway drug. But instead of forging ahead to a kind of love so rare I couldn't even imagine it, I'd declared victory at the first gate.

"I have . . . work to do," I said.

"We. *We*."

She reached into her bag and removed a book.

"I've been seeing someone," she said. "A therapist. This afternoon, he gave me this. I marked it."

She put the book on the table. A hand on my shoulder. No kiss good-bye.

"This was good," she said, and left.

I picked up the book.

Milan Kundera. *The Book of Laughter and Forgetting*. A page had been turned down and a passage marked:

Every love relationship is based upon unwritten conventions rashly agreed upon by the lovers during the first weeks of their love. On the one hand, they are living a sort of dream; on the other, without realizing it, they are drawing up the fine print of their contracts like the most hard-nosed of lawyers. O lovers! Be wary during those perilous first days! If you serve the other party breakfast in bed, you will be obliged to continue same in perpetuity or face charges of animosity and treason!

If Kundera was right, love goes wrong at the very beginning. With innocent decisions, made with the best intentions. The flaws are baked into the relationship.

Change? We say we want to be different, to be better, but we don't want to change; we want to *be* changed—we want to download the app and let the device do it all for us.

Students were streaming in. Greetings exchanged. Banter with the bartender as beers were ordered. A man reading a novel and dabbing his eyes with a handkerchief? Must be a good book.

CHAPTER 35

And on the next day, another email came:

FROM: *Blair.Watkins@gmail.com*
TO: *David@DGLaw.com*
SUBJECT: *"You've got to keep thinking/ You can make it thru these waves"*

D—

You very smartly did not ask what "it" is like with Jean. You're not entitled to know. But if, going forward, we're smart enough not to keep big secrets from each other, I need to say something or the unexpressed curiosity will kill you.

Jean's life could not be more different than ours. In her refrigerator: champagne, yogurt, and probiotics (because yogurt alone does not, apparently, keep your gut pristine).

I'd cook for her, but she's not interested. So we go out for dinner. And in restaurants, men send us drinks and then come over to hit on us. Gay? Neither of us registers that way.

I've been invited to more conferences this year, and I've gone out of town twice. Let me tell you, it's even weirder sleeping alone in a hotel room than sharing a bed with a woman. Coming in from the airport the first time, I got confused and asked to be taken to Central Park West. Only when we stopped in front of our building did I realize I wasn't going "home."

But you want to know about the sex. Short answer: It's confusing.

I keep reaching for something that isn't there. Toulouse-Lautrec often painted lesbians. He was a friend to many. Watching them sleep, arms and legs entwined, he wrote, "This is superior to everything. Nothing can compare to something so simple."

Nothing? He was on the outside, doing that male gaze thing.

On the inside? Nothing is that simple. I wish it were. Start the countdown.

Every word thrilled, the almost explicit message most of all.

The leaves had turned, and Blair had too—she wasn't going to spend forty-two days with Jean.

She'd be home soon.

The subject line was confirmation.

It was from "Blue," by Joni Mitchell, one of Blair's favorites. I knew it well. And what followed:

Blue, here is a shell for you
Inside you'll hear a sigh
A foggy lullaby
There is your song from me.

"A foggy lullaby"—it wasn't late, but I wanted to go to bed, to imagine Blair's good-night kiss, the day's last declaration of love, her warm breath in my ear. In the dark, I'd remember all the nights behind us and hope for the ones ahead. I'd recall cool sheets in summer, hiding under the duvet in winter, my hand massaging her shoulders as foreplay, her hair streaming across the pillow as she slept.

I wanted to respond but didn't trust myself not to fill a page. I'd been listening to a lot of blues and soul—what a surprise—and I kept coming back to Otis Redding, who was all man and all emotion. Before I thought about it, I hit Reply and typed the title of one of his songs:

"I've Been Loving You Too Long (to Stop Now)"

CHAPTER 36

But Blair didn't come home.

I read her email a dozen times, and I never failed to extract the message I wanted. She hadn't sent a hint, a wish, a statement of intent; the email was an affirmation of a contract. Of a new contract. Starting well before Thanksgiving. That the contract lacked a start date—I overlooked that.

So I was hopeful on October 29, jumpy on October 30, and agitated on October 31.

Halloween night: the worst. Ours is a small building by Manhattan standards—four apartments per floor, with just a dozen floors—but I would have sworn the bell rang a hundred times. Each time I opened the door, I expected to see Blair, and every time it was some grinning kid from the building.

"Cool costumes," I told the first callers as I doled out the candy I congratulated myself for remembering to buy. But soon I was offering candy in smaller amounts, saying nothing, annoyed that so few had charity boxes to fill with coins for the poor.

Then it was over, and I sat drinking rum and Coke—a quick high and a certain headache, not that I cared about anything but the high—by the window. The breeze felt like the tide coming in on a quiet summer night. By my second drink, I was almost content. And definitely buzzed.

The bell rang. Intrusive. Irritating. But there was candy left, and I still had the faintest hope Blair would be there with arms open, so I answered it.

"May I?" Jean asked, and breezed into the foyer without waiting for an answer.

I found myself a beat behind, nodding and closing the door. This was not right. I wished I'd had less to drink.

"Where's Blair?" I asked, not exactly blocking the hall but not exactly welcoming her in.

"The loft."

"Where does she think you are?"

"The parade."

Of course. The Greenwich Village Halloween parade. Mardi Gras for gays. Better: Carnival. Floats. Puppets. And fifty thousand people, many in costume. Blair would have assumed—or Jean would have told her—she was going there.

"Blair didn't go?" I asked.

"Not her thing. You'll be pleased to hear: Blair's not cut out for the gay life. Or even downtown."

"Why doesn't she come home?"

"I've asked her. I don't know."

"Pride," I suggested.

"Maybe. She's full of good qualities I don't seem to appreciate."

I could have been thrilled. Should have been. But rage surfaced—I hated that Jean knew Blair well enough to understand her.

A verbal sneer: "Perhaps your appeal wasn't to her good qualities."

"You're drinking," Jean said.

"Rum and coke. I'd offer you one, but that would be a friendly gesture."

"Well, I'm here as a friend."

"That worked with the doorman," I said. "It doesn't with me."

Jean had faced down icebergs and volcanoes. A boozy lawyer on Central Park West wasn't capable of delivering an insult that knocked her off her purpose.

"I'm here as a friend who wanted to see you one last time."

"Promise?"

She pulled a small, thin package wrapped in brown paper from her bag.

"And I brought you a present."

What could I say? I stepped aside, and Jean walked in. I followed, a security guard who suspects the worst.

At the end of the hall, she had a choice.

To her left was the living room, dark except for two small lamps. I grew up in a home with a TV set in every room; one of the pleasures of this apartment was having a living room without one. Blair and I used to spend evenings here, books in hand, drinks. Since she left, I'd avoided this room; it looked like a set for a show that had closed.

To the right was the dining room, lined with bookshelves. The table told the story: This was home base, everything I might want—computer, books, liquor—within easy reach. Dimmers worked overtime here, but at least it wasn't a chamber of despair, so Jean wandered in. I followed.

"Let's not prolong this," I said, and held out my hand.

Jean handed me the present. I wanted to play it cool and set it down, unopened, as if it were a trifle that could wait until later. But I wasn't that cool—I ripped the paper off.

It was a black-and-white photograph. Of Blair, naked to the top curve of her breasts, eyes wide open, staring directly into the camera. The twin to the picture that Jean had taken of herself and given to us.

"It's . . ." The sentence died there. No adjective conveyed my appreciation of the picture's beauty or Blair's willingness to drop every defense for Jean's camera or—and this is what stopped me—the indisputable fact that this was a photograph of a woman I knew very well and not at all.

Jean turned her attention from me to a book of Helmut Newton photographs on the table. I'd been looking through this book for a reason Jean could never have guessed: Although Newton's models were tall, leggy, and small-breasted, they reminded me of her. Tough. Clear-eyed. Unapologetic. Perverse. When I wanted to imagine what Blair and Jean were like together—I mean in bed—this book was the springboard for my fantasies.

"A lovely man," Jean said, running her hand over the cover.

"Seriously?"

"Not in his books . . . but there's a picture of Helmut on his deathbed. His wife is holding his head. It's just . . ."

Jean closed her eyes.

"You okay?" I asked, hoping, for my sake, that I was the only one on the edge of a large, messy emotion.

"That's a picture I'd love for someone to take of me—and no one ever will."

"You don't know that."

"Oh, David, you are such a child."

"The future's not a straight line."

"I'll see someone I want for a lover, and he'll stick around?"

"Or she will," I said.

"Like Blair?"

"Like someone."

"Never gonna happen."

"Why not?"

"Because I want a man. And when a woman hits forty, she becomes . . . invisible to men."

"No one could overlook you," I said.

"You did."

"Then."

"Tonight too." She whispered, but her whisper was urgent: "Look at me, David. Like you were taking my picture. Please."

So I did.

Tonight Jean was wearing a white men's dress shirt and faded Levis. Under the shirt, she had on a black tank top. You see this look all over New York, and on one of the last warm nights of the fall, it made sense.

But Jean did nothing the way other women did. And the difference was critical.

No bra.

Jean wasn't wearing a bra, and the tank top was made of some stretch fabric, and there, in outline, I could see her nipples. I might have noticed them earlier. Now I made up for that inattention by staring unashamedly.

Jean's breasts seemed bigger, fuller than I remembered. I pictured her displaying them, offering them, hands crossed underneath as she gently pulled on her nipples. I pictured her leaning over me, teasing my mouth. I pictured her . . .

Her gaze was steady and knowing. The tank top wasn't a casual choice. She hadn't "forgotten" to wear a bra.

"One last time," she whispered. "To say good-bye." Yes, and to get what she wanted when we met. To make me betray my understanding with Blair. And, surely, to get even with Blair for not falling in love with her.

These motives were clear to me. But they were less compelling than Jean's breasts. They were both concealed and revealed, which is always incendiary.

Was I a child? More like a teenager. The moment seemed to expand.

Jean took a deep breath.

I believed her breasts were pleading to me.

We kissed, hard and deep. Her shirt was discarded, then her tank top. Breasts were honored but in haste. In thrall to urgent, dirty, backseat-of-the-convertible sex, the floor was our certain destination.

I pulled away—I don't know how, but I did—and stood there, panting. As was Jean.

"The room is spinning," I said, and eased myself into a chair.

She smiled. "Again?"

Jean went to the kitchen. She returned, carrying water. She held the glass while I sipped. I leaned back. She dressed, kissed me gently on the top of my head, and I fell asleep. And then she was gone.

It was just ten when I woke up. Still Halloween. The night beckoned.

Out I went, into the park. It felt like paradise: pools of light, trees in silhouette, and the occasional falling leaf. As I walked around the reservoir toward Fifth Avenue, I fell in with Halloween revelers who also seemed to cherish big sky and open water in the center of the city. We made an unlikely circus troupe, with me, in a business shirt and jeans, the most unlikely.

Some kids were singing on the steps of the Met, but the

rest of Fifth Avenue, from the East 80s to the Apple cube, was deserted. I walked down to an Italian restaurant on Madison that was filled with buffed, painted women and aimless men in loafers without socks who didn't mind paying $300 for a bottle of champagne. I knew no one. I didn't want a hookup. Amid frivolity, I drank in peace.

At some point, it seemed like a good idea to breathe fresh air and call my wife. Leaving the restaurant was easy. Dialing a number was a challenge.

"Happy Halloween."

Not that Halloween was a holiday Blair and I celebrated.

"David? Where are you?"

"On Madison Avenue. Looking for the straight parade."

"Are you okay?"

"If 'drunk' is okay, I am beyond awesome."

This moment lacked precedent. Silence from Blair.

I remembered my reason for this call. "When are you coming home?"

"David, please . . ."

"Fuck 'please.' Enough, Blair. Come home."

"Soon. I'll be there soon. Really."

Her tone was soothing. I couldn't argue with her.

"Good," I whispered. I stood, phone to my head, wondering why I was putting her through this.

"Can someone find a cab for you?"

"I can get home."

"Me too," she said.

Again, I heard a promise but not a date. A cab stopped in front of the restaurant. A woman stepped out. I didn't merit a first glance. I took the cab.

CHAPTER 37

I would have preferred the park, but smoking anywhere in Central Park is now a crime. So when early November brought the last of the warm weather and the gaudiest of foliage, I took to sitting on a Fifth Avenue bench after work, reading and thinking and smoking a cigar.

After work one warm afternoon, I sat for hours. There was some kind of cocktail party or book party or charity launch in a townhouse just off Fifth, and as it ended, guests who hadn't come in town cars started toward the avenue to flag taxis. I didn't know all of them, but through clients and lawyer gossip and years of just being around, I had intimate knowledge of many of these A-listers. And I saw them with a terrible clarity.

The CEO who lived at the Carlyle with his mistress. At

seven thirty most weekday mornings, you could see him leave the hotel to walk his dog. But that walk led only across the street, because when you have a suspicious wife in bed upstairs and another lover across town, it's better to drop coins into a pay phone than create a cell phone record that could become evidence.

I saw the real estate czar who had announced at a party, "If you have less than seven hundred and fifty million dollars, you have no hedge against inflation." Then came the crash of 2008, and he had no hedge. He had even less when his wife divorced him and took nearly half of what was left. But he had the great good luck to marry an otherworldly heiress who wouldn't sign the prenup he had us write for him because it was, she said, "too long." Now the gods had made her ill, and he was doing a good impression of a man who didn't care that a marital tragedy would put a fresh billion in his bank account.

I saw the copper king whose Bolivian mines created mounds of waste. The wind sent lead and arsenic from that waste airborne while slagheaps dripped those poisons into lakes, where Bolivian children eat the fish and breathe the air, and you don't want to think about the sicknesses there. The copper king had brought his son, a teenager in a school blazer. The boy looked smart, healthy, and decent, but as I considered his criminal of a father, I pictured the kid as a Bolivian teenager, ravaged by disease. And that felt like justice to me.

Ah, a correspondent for a network news magazine and his new wife. V and I represented his first wife in their divorce. She told us a story of her husband working on a piece in Kansas, calling her to check in, then going on to his next call—only there was a glitch, and she didn't get disconnected, so she had the pleasure of hearing him chat up some bimbo, repeating tidbits he'd just delivered to her. The secret of life is repeat business; I looked forward to representing the new wife.

And here was the serial entrepreneur and his society wife, standing on the corner, looking for their driver. Blair and I had been at a dinner party they gave to celebrate the opening of yet another restaurant. (They actually used that word: *celebrate*. Like a restaurant was a milestone.) We were the poorest people there by about $500 million. Several guests had just bought brownstones. They're quite the rage these days, and expensive; anybody who wants to spend less than $20 million is talking Brooklyn. When the entrepreneur said he had a construction crew—nonunion, Chinese—he'd be happy to loan to them, these people were beside themselves with delight. And I thought: How are the rich different from you and me? They're cheaper.

And why was I not surprised to see Billy and Nancy Robb Russakof? Arm in arm, they turned the corner and started walking home to their penthouse. A very happy couple. Well, she had every reason to make him think so. Better to have all the frequent flyer miles than to fight for half.

These people were like middle-aged fashion models, cosmetically flawless, with warehouses of smiles to share with one another. In a city where diversity is our greatest asset, they had turned their backs on it and formed a village, separated from the rest of us by a thick wall of money.

They knew only one god and one law: Don't lose your fortune.

Let the record show that I have carried water for these people, flattered them, and made good on all promises to them. One on one, I like them, or at least have enough compassion not to sneer. But sitting on that bench, watching a gang of them, I hated them.

Not for long.

Ten minutes later, when all the guests had drifted out and the hosts were driven to an even more elite event, I saw my city—and my place in it—through new eyes. The windows of the great apartment buildings, dark all summer, now glowed. Women wore scarves. Blair was, at most, days away. V and I were in sync. My happiness—the possibility of it, the fresh start, atonement—awaited only a time stamp.

I set my iPhone for random music, inserted my ear buds, and listened as I walked. There was even some striding—give me a crisp drummer and a bass player with wit, and I have to resist the urge to dance.

Then I was served a song I knew well: "Joy to You Baby," by Josh Ritter.

The song came with a story, and because it was one of Blair's favorites, I knew it. A year after he married another musician, Ritter was on tour, in some godforsaken hotel in some distant city, when his wife called and ended the marriage. He was crushed. All he could do was write, and that he did—boxes of bitter, angry verses.

I don't know how he fought his way out of that gloom, but he did, and in this song, his only wish is joy—joy to the city, joy to the streets, the freeway, the cars, and "joy to you baby, wherever you are tonight." Joy to his ex-wife? Yes. Even her.

I thought: We can set the rope down. It has been done. It can be done. I can do it.

As a thought exercise, I mouthed the words: *Jean, thank you for standing in my way. Blair, I will learn to see you as you are.* And the hardest: *David, I forgive you.*

I walked uptown on Fifth, to that point beyond the museums where the money is quiet and elegance is earned. A black car stopped at the awning of a limestone apartment building. A doorman hurried to greet it. Ralph Lauren stepped out and shook the doorman's hand. Not a required gesture, just a very human one. Something he did. Something he probably did every night.

I liked that. It was just the kind of anecdote I wanted to tell Blair.

CHAPTER 38

In Mongolia, when a baby cries, every woman in the room opens her blouse and shakes her breasts, and the baby smiles and stops crying.

I read that on the Internet, so it must be true.

I read a lot on the Internet that first week in November.

A tasty Thanksgiving turkey requires a night in a saltwater bath. I knew nothing about brining. Now that I do, I will not fail to brine our turkeys.

Bruce Springsteen called his mother when he signed his first recording contract. His mother's response: "So what did you change your name to?"

The Supreme Court has its own, regulation-size basketball court. They call it "the highest court in the land."

Mick Jagger and Keith Richards were not the founders of

the Rolling Stones. The founders were Brian Jones, who died a few years later, and Ian Stewart, a great piano player who, the band's manager decided, had the wrong look. After he was fired, Stewart became the Stones' road manager. He died, at forty-seven, of a heart attack in the office of his cardiologist.

I could go on . . .

Mostly, I kept my head down and worked steadily during the day.

At night, I kept my head sober and the apartment pristine.

And then, later at night, I thought of my reunion with Blair.

Running the reservoir in the morning, passing the south steps, and there, at the top of the stairs . . . Blair.

A woman who says she needs a divorce lawyer makes an appointment. Victoria refers her to me. I assume she's sixty. She enters . . . Blair.

Blair and I support WFUV, the local alternative rock radio station. They're sponsoring a small acoustic concert with our favorite singer-songwriter. I arrive early. Someone tapes a RESERVED sign on the seat next to me. Just before the lights dim, a woman removes the sign . . . Blair.

I'm writing an article for the Style section of the Sunday *Times* about cheaters' websites. The angle is the predictability of the men; many look for women who are like their wives, just sleeker. To gather information, I sign up for one. Purely for journalistic purposes, I suggest a meeting with a woman who reminds me of Blair. When we meet . . . Blair.

Reboot calls to tell me he's found something I should see. I rush to the fountain overlooking the pond in Central Park. Waiting for me . . . Blair.

A hostess sends an invitation for a dinner party. I reply that I'll be coming solo. When I arrive . . . Blair.

Or the ultimate: the beach. I'm walking, swathed in despair. In the distance, coming toward me, a woman. Can it be? I walk faster. She walks faster. Then we're running but in slow motion. We strain. We pump. Music swells. I fall into her arms . . . Blair.

What *actually* happened? It was early evening. The World Series had finally ended. A Kenyan with a beautiful smile had won the marathon. Piles of leaves in the park. Sweaters. Stews and short ribs on restaurant menus. Bordeaux on display in the wine store.

And I was out of milk.

On Central Park West, walking back from the deli, I saw a woman coming toward me who looked like Blair. Walked like Blair. Pulling a suitcase. Had a large bag over her shoulder just like Blair's.

We met in front of our building.

She was crying. But not as hard as I was.

A wordless hug. Fierce. On both sides, fierce.

"We were out of milk," I said, very aware of the plural.

"I'll make coffee," she said.

We walked into the lobby together, murmuring good evening to the doorman as if there was nothing unusual about tenants he hadn't seen together for more than a month greeting him with tears streaming down their faces and smiling.

In the elevator, I grabbed Blair, held her tight.

Then, because that seemed too fast, too premature, I let her go.

We stood in the elevator, not touching, looking at each other. The door closed. Neither of us moved to press a button.

It's possible to communicate without speaking, and in the way we were looking at each other, we were doing that—shifting the power, letting the scales balance, finding where we were and starting there. But words seal understanding, and we knew what they were and how simple.

The words were about compassion and tolerance and not running away from discomfort. We stood together and whispered them to each other. I pressed the button. We started to rise.

Then Blair took a step, and I took a step, and we held each other.

ACKNOWLEDGMENTS

This book was conceived several presidents ago, put on hold while I had a 24/7 job, and periodically pushed to the side by life events, so the support of friends has been crucial. I'm grateful to the community that makes Head-Butler.com possible, especially the 125 readers who made their way through an early draft and offered suggestions. At Open Road, where I've had an experience that writers dream of, I am beyond indebted to Jane Friedman, Tina Pohlman, Sarah Yurch, Laura De Silva, and my impeccable editor, Maggie Crawford. I thank Alan Sacks for legal advice delivered in a South African accent. Others who cheered me on include Pamela Barr, Geraldine Baum, Louise Bernikow, Carroll Bogert, Michael Bush, Marshall Cohen, David Patrick Columbia, Frank Delaney, Julie Du Brow,

Pimm Fox, Justin Frank, Christina Green Gerry, Wendy Goldberg, Beth Gutcheon, Stephen Hanan, Paul Hoppe, Erin Johnson, Bob Jeffrey, Tsipi Keller, Craig Lambert, Susan Lehman, Diane Meier, Kriena Nederveen, Donna Paul, Judy Resnick, Colette Rhoney, Bob Sabbag, Marian Salzman, Kate Seward, Sheila Weller, and Kitty Wise. Special thanks to friends who went above and beyond: Renata Adler, Dominique Browning, Gretl Claggett, Carol Fitzgerald, Joy Frelinghuysen, Alison Franklin, Julie Metz, N. E. Lasater, Esther Perel, and Paige Peterson. Many thanks to Bob Pittman and Ken Lerer, who hired me at AOL and, in essence, provided the writing fellowship that made this book possible. Thanks to Liane Reed, Richard Kornbluth, and Pearl Kornbluth for never suggesting I might be casting shame on the family. And, most of all, to my wife, for her saintly tolerance, and our teenage daughter, for her total disdain.

ABOUT THE AUTHOR

Jesse Kornbluth is the founder of HeadButler.com, a cultural concierge site. He has served as editorial director of AOL, cofounded Bookreporter.com, and was a contributing editor to *Vanity Fair*, *New York*, and *Architectural Digest*. The author of four nonfiction books, including *Highly Confident: The Crime and Punishment of Michael Milken*, he has written screenplays for Paul Newman, Robert De Niro, ABC, PBS, and Warner Bros.

Married Sex is Kornbluth's first novel. He lives in Manhattan with his family.

OPEN ROAD
INTEGRATED MEDIA

Open Road Integrated Media is a digital publisher and multimedia content company. Open Road creates connections between authors and their audiences by marketing its ebooks through a new proprietary online platform, which uses premium video content and social media.

CPSIA information can be obtained at www.ICGtesting.com
Printed in the USA
BVOW08s1156150715

408215BV00002B/2/P